A BOOK JUST FOR ME

My Brother Dan's Delicious

Steven L. Layne

Illustrated by Chuck Galey

PELICAN PUBLISHING COMPANY

GRETNA 2007

To Sandy, for keeping the faith—S. L. L.

To W. E. Galey, Jr.—Daddy

First printing, January 2003
Second printing, October 2004
Third printing, August 2007

*The word "Pelican" and the depiction of a pelican are trademarks
of Pelican Publishing Company, Inc., and are registered
in the U.S. Patent and Trademark Office.*

Library of Congress Cataloging-in-Publication Data

Layne, Steven L.
  My brother Dan's delicious / Steven L. Layne ; illustrated by Chuck Galey.
      p. cm.
Summary: When he finds that he is home alone for the first time, a bright
eight-and-a-half-year-old boy informs any monsters that might be lurking in
the house that his older brother Dan is worth the wait.
  ISBN-13: 978-1-58980-071-7 (alk. paper)
  [1. Monsters—Fiction. 2. Brothers—Fiction. 3. Fear—Fiction.] I.
Galey, Chuck, ill. II. Title.
  PZ7.L44675 My 2003
  [Fic]—dc21
                                            2002008380

Printed in Singapore
Published by Pelican Publishing Company, Inc.
1000 Burmaster Street, Gretna, Louisiana 70053

My Brother Dan's Delicious

Sometimes, when you're eight and a half, life throws you an unexpected curve. In my case, it happened just last night. I went to my best friend Dave's house for supper, and his mother served one of her weird casseroles. It looked to me like things were moving underneath the crust, so I didn't eat much. I left his house at seven o'clock, walked three blocks to my house, and that's where all the trouble started. When I reached our front door, I found a note.

Dear Joey,
Your father and I went across the street to have a cup of coffee with the Dicksons. Dan is at the movies with a friend, but he will be home soon.

Love,
Mom

At first glance, the note did not appear to be a problem. In fact, I was thrilled! My mother and father were finally admitting that their youngest child, a member of the gifted and talented class at Horace E. Depworth Elementary School, was old enough to stay home alone.

At second, third, and fourth glance, however, I became rather upset. I mean, *What was the matter with my parents?* This note was advertising to practically the *entire world* that an innocent youngster, not to mention the child voted most interesting Show-and-Tell speaker for three years running, was going to be left home *alone* and *unprotected*.

Now everyone knows that monsters, especially those with a taste for pan-fried boys, are waiting for just this kind of opportunity to come along.

Of course, I'm too old to believe in them anymore, but if I *did* still believe in monsters, you can be sure I'd know just how to handle this type of situation.

The first step, of
course, is to get inside the
house, where your movements
cannot be easily tracked. The second
step is to identify the likely hiding
places of these villainous creatures if, in
fact, they are already inside the house. The third
and most important step in dealing with
monsters, however, is to *distract*
them.

For example, if I felt that a monster was watching me at this very moment, thinking perhaps about a fantastic dinner featuring Joseph A. Demorett II as the main course, I would simply alert him to the existence of my older, larger, *tastier* brother Dan!

There are times when sacrifice is the only way. I would miss him, but he *does* have the bigger bedroom.

Perhaps, for the benefit of those who still give in to that occasional moment of "monster fear," I should begin a demonstration.

Are there any monsters about? If there are, I just want you to know, my brother Dan's *delicious!* Yes, indeedy-do. He's one ultratasty guy. He's a succulent sibling, all right. Any monsters looking for a tender boy to munch on would do well to stay right where you are while I share some personal insights on what makes my brother a magnificent meal choice.

Well, to begin with, Dan's a big guy. Sort of. Okay, so he didn't make the wrestling team, and Lisa Jean Owen beat him up a few times. Still, he's bigger than I am.

I mean, a guy like me would barely make an appetizer; whereas a monster who planned well could probably get at least three good meals out of Dan!

Do I hear the sounds of stomach growling coming from behind that basement door? Well, just you *stay put!*

My brother Dan will be home soon; my brother Dan's *delicious!*

Next, let's consider intake. Danny-boy eats all of the stuff Mom tells him to—carrots, potatoes . . . even broccoli! A guy like me prefers goodies from the candy counter at Mrs. Castelli's Drugstore. I buy them in secret, eat them in secret, and then tell Mom I'm not hungry at dinnertime. So, any monster with dietary concerns is going to want to grab Danny. He's like a Thanksgiving turkey already stuffed for the platter!

Is something smacking its lips with eager anticipation inside that coat closet? Well, just you *stay put!* My brother Dan will be home soon; my brother Dan's *delicious!*

In most of the stories I've read, monsters have all kinds of trouble capturing the boys they want to eat. But in Danny's case, a smart monster will meet with easy success *and* have a good laugh before dinner. In other words, Dan's not too bright.

Some boys, on the other hand, would be much more difficult to capture. These persons would be characterized as receiving top scores on national achievement tests as well as being the one Mrs. Biggs chooses to take messages to the office and whom she may secretly want to marry someday.

So why be depressed and disappointed trying to outsmart an intellectual giant when I can simply tell Dan it's a costume party and dress him as a pot roast?

Is something about to release some terribly discolored saliva from underneath that king-sized bed? Well, just you *stay put!* My brother Dan will be home soon; my brother Dan's *delicious!*

Finally, and most importantly, there's the issue of *taste*. Fortunately, I can offer personal testimony to the fact that my brother Dan is nothing less than a thirteen-year-old, mouthwatering flavor factory!

It *is* true that I came by this knowledge through a rather painful series of events that found Dan's hands and feet colliding with my mouth at a force just below nuclear. Still, I must confess that in each and every one of those situations, I noticed that my brother had a uniquely appetizing taste.

Wha . . . wha . . . what's that giant shadow moving just outside the back-porch door? Well, just you *stay put!*

My brother Dan will be home soon; my brother Dan's *delicious!* Yes, my brother Dan's *delicious, divine, delectable,* and *delightful!* He's a meaty, mouthwatering meal of undeniable flavor. Yes! He's an unparalleled taste sensation. He's . . . uh . . . uh . . . a virtual *banquet* for monsters of our day!

Hey! I know! I know! When he arrives, I'll signal any waiting monsters with a secret code sentence. Okay? Then, he's all yours! As soon as I get him into position, I'll yell really loud, *"My brother Dan's . . .*

MY HERO!"

She's a master class in song writing, and I've always been in love with the teacher.

Del Bryant

In my life I have had the opportunity to spend a great deal of time with many entertainers and performers, not to mention politicians and public figures. Although most of them are good people, very few stand out as being great in the heart, where it really matters. As if she were cut from the stone of the Kentucky Mountains she was reared in, Loretta Lynn is one of these real and forthright folks, nothing forced or faked about her character. She is the genuine "real deal," and what you see is what you get. My parents were this type of people, and knowing them as well as I did, as I have gotten close to Loretta over the past few years, I have determined her to be the same—sincere, straightforward, and open. She is a treasure to our world of music; that much should go without saying. But to me she is so much more. She is the living embodiment and a reminder of the fact that greatness does not come from an illusion but from an honest and truly good heart. Shine on, Loretta; I am blessed to have known you.

John Carter Cash

HONKY TONK GIRL

HONKY TONK GIRL

MY LIFE IN LYRICS

Loretta Lynn

ALFRED A. KNOPF · NEW YORK · 2012

THIS IS A BORZOI BOOK
PUBLISHED BY ALFRED A. KNOPF

Library of Congress Cataloging-in-Publication Data
Lynn, Loretta.
[Lyrics]
Honky tonk girl : my life in lyrics / by Loretta Lynn. — First edition.
pages   cm
ISBN: 978-0-307-59489-1
1. Country music—Texts.   I. Title.
ML54.6.L89H66   2012
782.421642'0268—dc23
2011050759

Jacket photograph by Russ Harrington, courtesy of the Loretta Lynn Foundation
Jacket design by Carol Devine Carson

Manufactured in the United States of America
First Edition

To me, my life has always been a song.

This book of my songs I dedicate

to my late husband, Doolittle, and our children,

Betty, Jack, Ernest, Cissie, Peggy, and Patsy.

Foreword

I am sitting at a wooden table in the cabin in Hendersonville waiting for Loretta to arrive. I'd been here before, visiting Johnny Cash in 1981. My autograph is among those carved into the "visitors' book" on a raw wooden beam above the stone fireplace.

Today, John Carter Cash is working on some new recordings in the studio that now adjoins the older structure. I've already overdubbed a harmony part on Loretta's fine versions of a Todd Snider song and my own tune, "Down Among the Wines and Spirits," which has been arranged in the likeness of an old Ray Price record.

I'm shuffling through some papers and a handful of changes, looking for a starting place to propose, when the door swings open. Miss Loretta comes in like a whirlwind of laughter and greetings. We get straight to work.

There isn't time to tell her how the first song I cut with Billy Sherrill, back in '81, was based on her rendition of Hank Cochran's "She's Got You." Well, we changed one essential word and then went on to do a straight take on her song "Honky Tonk Girl."

Today is about new songs. Loretta produces a concertina file in which you might keep receipts or invoices. On it is a label that reads SONGS. Foolscap, legal yellow pad, telephone message pad paper, and notes scribbled on the backs of receipts all tumble out onto the table.

There are so many titles and opening lines that it is hard to know where to start. There are songs that should have been written but somehow haven't been, like "Thank God for Jesus."

How can that not exist?

One proposed title really stops me in my tracks. It was "I Felt the Chill Before the Winter Came." It seemed to contain already a whole story. Now we just had to trick it out.

I don't recall the order of what happened next. It seemed rapid and in slow motion at the same time. One image led to another, and, as with all viable songwriting collaborations, we were soon completing each other's thoughts and melodic lines.

I'm playing a J-200 that is as old as I am. The chords fall into place easily, but when the spacing or phrasing of cadence is not working, Loretta is on it like a flash. It ends up being characteristic of both our styles. We each took turns in singing the song, and in a short while the writing was complete.

The only lyrical difference between our two versions is the way I complete the bridge lines . . .

But I knew that we would go wrong
Just as they do in all of those tragic songs

I thought this might sound more believable coming from me than Loretta's original and true line.

Just as they do in those honky tonk songs

There just weren't that many honky tonks in either Twickenham or Liverpool, where I grew up, and there are fewer still in Vancouver and New York City, where I live. We pick another title and opening sketch from the pile. There is less in the way of a lyric than a description, something about a wronged woman meeting her rival.

I can tell that this one might take a little while to work out. I ask Loretta if I could make the title character into the biblical Eve and promise to send a draft when I'm done.

After sitting a good bit, talking thoughtfully and with full hearts about life, love, and family and laughing at mischievous things that Loretta says with love about some other singers, we go back to looking through the lyrics, titles, descriptions of songs, looking for a third starting place.

I pick up a piece of cardboard and realize that I am not staring at an unfinished or unreleased song but a first draft of one of Loretta's biggest hits—I want to say it was "You Ain't Woman Enough," but my memory might be deceiving me. But it really was a song that famous.

I said, "Shouldn't this be in the Country Music Hall of Fame?"

Loretta laughed at the idea and turned the piece of cardboard over. It had been torn off the packaging from an item of underwear and must have been all that was available when inspiration struck. Thank goodness for cardboard.

"Oh, I see," I said, slightly embarrassed at the intrusion. "I suppose then they'd know all your secrets."

Now it was time for Loretta to fix one line that had dropped out on a live recording. I was gathering up our various drafts as Loretta slipped into the vocal booth. As I was closing my guitar case, I heard what I took to be a tape of the flawed live recording.

Looking up, I saw it was actually Loretta delivering a first-take performance that few singers could achieve without an hour of warm-up. No preparation, no warning. She is right there when the red light goes on.

Elvis Costello
New York City, March 2011

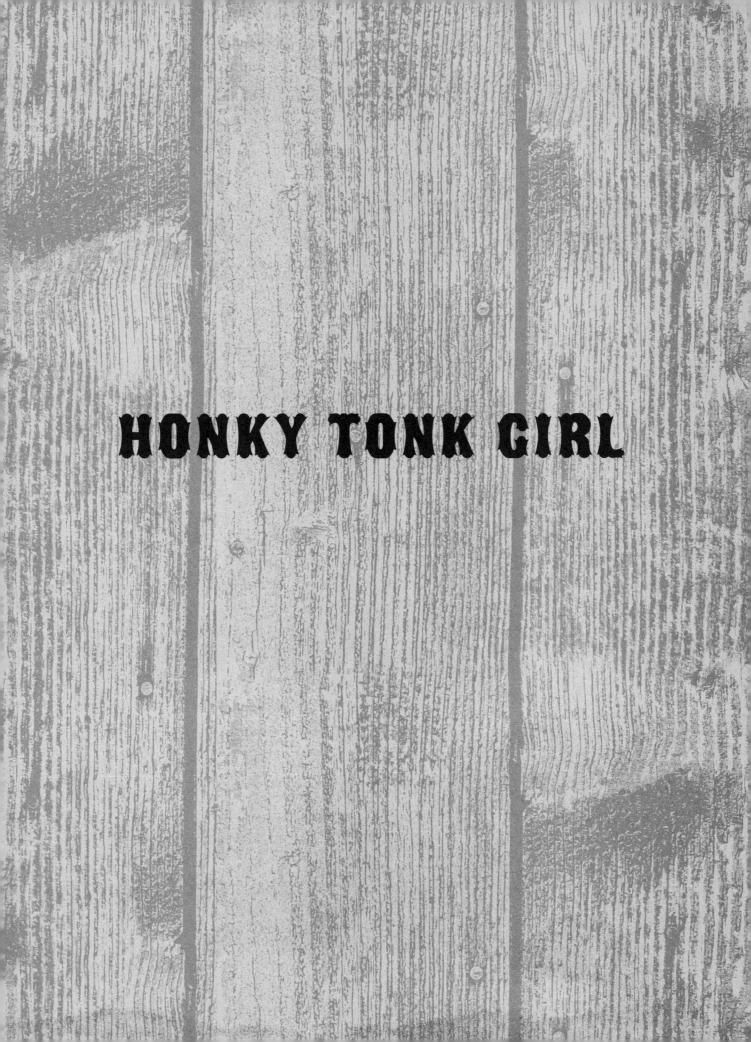

HONKY TONK GIRL

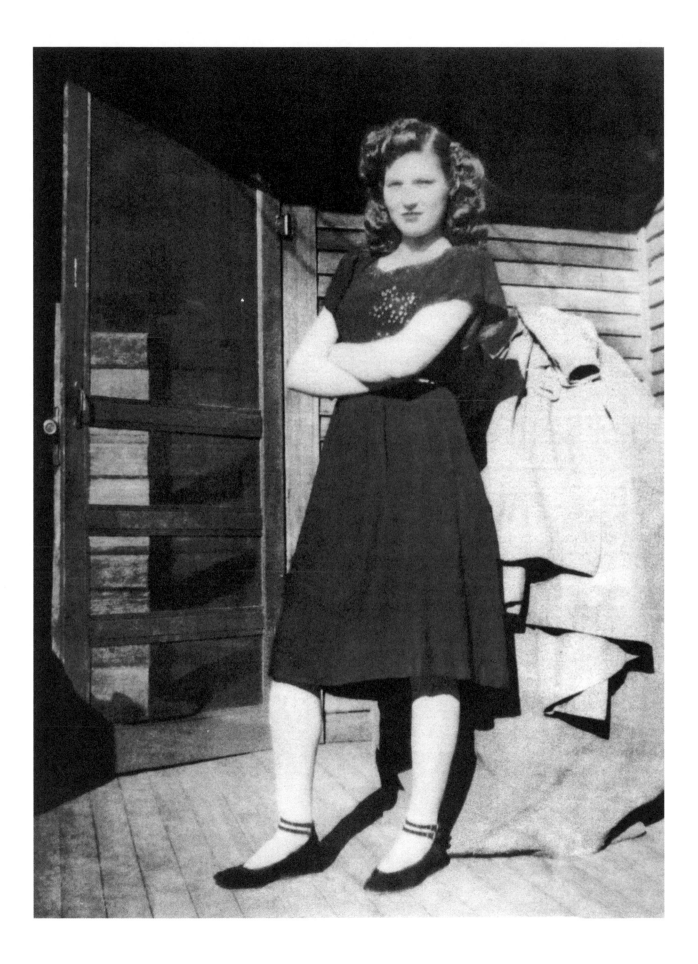

Introduction

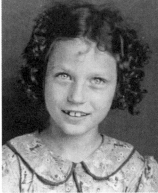

This is me. Loretta.

And this whole book is me, too. These lyrics cover fifty years of my sittin' down with my pencil and my guitar and writing about my life.

As I write this, I've just survived a flood and tornadoes in Hurricane Mills, Tennessee. I've survived a lot of things in my lifetime. And I guess that's what most of these songs are about: survivin'.

I wrote my very first lyric when I wrote "Whispering Sea." It wound up being the B-side of "Honky Tonk Girl." Me and my husband were livin' in the state of Washington, and one day we went fishing. I don't know why I just sat down and wrote a song. But I remember being shocked that those lyrics just came pourin' out of me. I also remember how excited I was. And you know what? I get that

same sense of excitement when I write a song today. It's just as strong as it was then. And it stirs up just as much emotion.

Whatever I feel that day and that moment, that's what I write. I put my whole heart and soul and body into my writing. I write about how I feel and what I am. I guess I never need to go to a psychiatrist—'cause I get everything out in my lyrics. I guess when you boil it all down, every song is

LEFT Loretta, nine years old
BELOW AND OPPOSITE Loretta, teen years

about me. It's my eyes that are seein' what I write about. And my heart that's feelin' all those things.

I think the saddest song I ever wrote was "This Haunted House," right after Patsy Cline passed away. I was over at her house and then went into the driveway and wrote the song. And strangely enough, the song that maybe makes me the happiest is "Two Steps Forward and Six Steps Back Again." That's a real old one—probably close to fifty years old—and I don't know why I think it's happy, 'cause it's all about cheatin'. But I just love singing it.

I guess I've written everything in between those two songs, too. As I said, I'm writing about me and my life, and life ain't simple all the time. Like the songs, life is happy and sad and all that stuff in between.

I feel good that I've written so many songs. I'm a little amazed that I've been doin' it as long as I have. And looking back on all these lyrics made me realize several things. One is that there ain't nothing in life that brings me as much joy as writing. I'd rather write than sing, even though I haven't written much over the past couple of years. But the good thing about doing this book is it made me realize how much I want to keep writing. So that's what I'm going to do from here on.

I hope that all the songs—the ones in this book and the ones I'm going to write in the future—make people as happy as they make me.

Loretta Lynn
Hurricane Mills, May 2011

"The Story of My Life"

I wrote the song "The Story of My Life" just because I was born in old Kentucky in them hills where folks are lucky!

I wrote this song in about 1959. It was one of my first ones. Doo and I'd just started, and I was learning how to write songs. For me, I could and can only write what I've lived. I recorded this song on my very first session on Zero Records and forgot about it! My daughter and biggest fan, Patsy, on the other hand, didn't. She loved it, drug it out, and wrote a couple of new verses to it, played it for Jack White, and the rest is history. Now I can forget about this song again (laughing)!

Here's the story of my life,
Listen close and I'll tell ya twice.
Yeah hey, yeah hey, yeah hey.

I was born in old Kentucky
In them hills where folks are lucky
And it's paradise to me.
Well, I got a feller right over the hill
If he asks me to marry well I know
   I will.

He asked me to marry, got kids of
   four
And I'm tellin' you I don't want no
   more.
Yeah hey, yeah hey, yeah hey.

Doo got me a guitar, I wrote me a
   song
Moved to Nashville and it wasn't
   long
Till I was on the Grand Ole Opry.

We bought us a mansion on the hill
Livin' big like we were big deals
Scarlett O'Hara, *Gone With the
   Wind*

I was pregnant again.
Oh gee, oh Lord I swear
The babies are comin' in pairs.
Yeah hey, yeah hey, yeah hey.

Well, some big shot from
   Hollywood
Thought a movie about my life
   would be good
It was a big hit, made a big splash
What I wanna know is what
   happened to the cash.
Yeah hey, yeah hey, yeah hey.

Now me and Doo married forty-
   eight years
Six kids later, a lot of laughter and
   tears.
I have to say that I've been blessed
Not bad for this old Kentucky girl I
   guess.
Yeah hey, yeah hey, yeah hey.
Yeah hey, yeah hey, yeah hey.

Well, here's the story of my life,
Listen and I'll tell it twice.
Yeah hey, yeah hey, yeah hey . . .

Wilburns

If it wasn't for Teddy and Doyle Wilburn, I don't know if I would have gotten to be as successful as I became in country music.

I met Doyle for the first time in 1960. I had just recorded my record *Honky Tonk Girl* on Zero label. We met at a DJ convention out west. I gave Doyle my record, and he gave me his address and told me if me and my husband ever got to Nashville we should let him know. As soon as I got home, I started writing the Wilburns letters. And they always wrote me back. I told them I really wanted to get my foot in the door in the music business. So Doyle and Teddy sent me out six songs and said to learn them and if I ever came to Nashville, Tennessee, they would demo me singing them. That was all we needed to hear! Me and Doo loaded our oldest off to Doo's mom and daddy, and Ernest and Cissie went to my mommy's house in Indiana ... then we drove straight to the Wilburn Brothers' office. Lord, them boys were surprised to see us.

The Wilburns were a big family, and the whole family worked there. They took me and Doo in, found us a place to stay, fed us, gave us money, and treated us like their family.

Teddy and Doyle did what they said they would do. I learned all the songs they sent me, and they cut my first demos. The boys and I became close, like sister and brothers. Teddy and Doyle were already pretty big stars in country music and really good businessmen. They started working with me, teaching me how to sing and how to think about writing songs so I could become a better songwriter. Heck, Teddy even bought me my first pair of high heels. He said that I came to Nashville looking like Annie Oakley's lost sister! I put on those high heels, and Teddy made me walk up and down the hallway at his office until I had blisters.

I wrote with both Teddy and Doyle. I had never written with anyone before, so it was like stepping into a whole new world. I learned so much from them. The boys said they were learning from me, too. Teddy and I spent the most time together, since he was the more musical of the two. Doyle was more of the manager type, at least when it came to working with me.

Both always encouraged me to write my own songs. They also got me signed to Decca Records, and they asked Owen Bradley to produce me. Later, the boys got their own TV show and asked me to be the girl singer on the show. Throughout the sixties and early seventies, they became my partners in songwriting, my publishers, and my managers. The whole family, from Lester to Leslie, kept our books and paid all our bills. Momma Wilburn became like a second mom to me and Doo.

All the Wilburns, like Doolittle, have passed away. But like my kids are now helping me run my business, their family is the same. Not too long ago, me and my kids and Arvimia Wilburn and her sons were all together. It was so great to see our children talking about songs and pitching songs and talking business. Just seeing them working together was great. I couldn't stop smiling. Family ...

"I'm a Honky Tonk Girl"

RELEASE DATE 1960

I always heard music when I was growing up, but writing a song is a bit different than just listening. In the mountains people would write about the things that happened, good or bad, so that's just what I did. I guess I had been singing three or four weeks when a girl I had picked strawberries with started coming in the little club where I worked. She would sit in the same booth every night. She never had drunk before, so after about two or three beers she would start to cry. One night on my ten-minute break I got down offstage and asked her why she was coming to the club alone and drinking. She told me her husband had left her and their seven children about three months ago for a younger woman who didn't live too far from where she lived. Then we both cried. That night I wrote this song about her. It was the first song I ever wrote.

Ever since you left me I've done
   nothing but wrong
Many nights I've laid awake and
   cried
We was so happy my heart was in
   a whirl

But now I'm a honky tonk girl
So turn that jukebox way up high
And fill my glass up while I cry
I've lost everything in this world
And now I'm a honky tonk girl

I just can't make a right with all
   of my wrongs
Every evening of my life seems so
   long
I'm sorry and ashamed for all these
   things you see
But losing him has made a fool of
   me
So fill my glass up to the brim
To lose my memory of him
I've lost everything in this world
And now I'm a honky tonk girl

Buck Owens

Out on the West Coast, Buck Owens was the biggest star in country music and he had his own TV show and talent contest. Doo decided I should enter Buck's contest. If you won, you got a wristwatch. You could pick a man's or a woman's watch. Well, I did win, so I got Doo a watch. Then I entered again and won me a watch! For years I gave Buck a hard time about these watches because both of them tore up in a week. I told him he gave cheap prizes!!

Buck and his wife at the time, Bon-

nie, became great friends of ours. I always loved Buck's music. He was a smart businessman, too. Starting out, Buck gave us a lot of valuable advice. When I recorded *Honky Tonk Girl*, I recorded it in a little studio in L.A. with the great Speedy West, and I didn't really understand that there was a difference in music sound depending on the areas. You have heard of people calling it "the Nashville sound." Well, there is a West Coast sound that is definitely not the same as the Nashville

sound. I think that my first record was a hit because it sounded so different from the other girl singers. It was a shuffle with a West Coast beat. I believe that's why folks liked it so much.

Buck Owens and Bonnie Owens stayed good friends of mine and Doo's for years. Buck said in an interview one time that he had a crush on me for years. That was really nice, but good thang Doolittle never heard that!

"Girl That I Am Now"

RELEASE DATE 1963
ALBUM *Loretta Lynn Sings*

Mhm mhm mhm oh could he love
　the girl that I am now
Tonight I'm in his arms but he just
　don't seem the same
I cheated and I'm guilty my heart
　can't stand this pain
I let passions fill my mind from my
　heart and conscience blind
I'm feelin' mighty low and I pray
　he'll never know
He loved the girl I used to be could
　he love the girl that I am now

It almost breaks my heart when he
　says that he loves me
I know that I'm not worthy and
　that's what troubles me
If he knew what I had done could
　he still feel just the same
Or would he feel the way I do guilty
　and ashamed
He loved the girl I used to be could
　he love the girl that I am now
Mhm mhm mhm oh could he love
　the girl that I am now

"Hundred Proof Heartache"

RELEASE DATE 1963
ALBUM *Loretta Lynn Sings*

I've got a hundred proof heartache
　and a case of the blues
My baby's gone and left me I've
　lost all I can lose
I've got a hundred proof heartache
　my world keeps turnin' round
This hundred proof heartache's got
　me down
You waded through my tears and
　said goodbye
You didn't seem to care how much
　I'd cry
You made your home the tavern
　down the street
And this old heart cries out with
　every beat
I've got a hundred proof heartache
　and a case of the blues
You're holdin' someone else tonight
　I just got the news
You left a hundred proof heartache
　for a love that's secondhand
This hundred proof heartache I
　can't stand

I've got a hundred proof heartache
　my world keeps turnin' round
This hundred proof heartache's got
　me down

Kitty Wells

My favorite singer in the world is Kitty Wells. She was the first girl singer to really break out on her own in country music and make a name for herself. When I first started really learning how to sing well, you can bet I learned every Kitty Wells song there was out. I tried my best to sound just like her, but I could never be as great as her. Listening to artists like Kitty Wells, Ernest Tubb, Hank Williams, Buck Owens, and studying their songs was how I think I learned to start writing. They made me understand how to meter words to a melody. If it wasn't for songs like "It Wasn't God Who Made Honky Tonk Angels," then there wouldn't be my first song, "Honky Tonk Girl." Singing Kitty songs, or any other well-known singer's songs, is fine when you're learning. But if you want to make a name for yourself then you have to make your own style. There can't be two Kitty Wellses.

Kitty Wells is not just my favorite singer, she's also my hero. Kitty is the queen of country music and she and her husband, Johnny, are great people. I am proud to call them my friends.

"World of Forgotten People"

RELEASE DATE 1963
ALBUM *Loretta Lynn Sings*

I live in a world world of
     forgotten people
Who've loved and lost their hearts
     so many times
I'm here in a world world of
     forgotten people
Where every heart is aching just
     like mine

Well I've loved and I've been loved
     but I had a reckless heart
And the many dreams I've had I've
     torn apart
Now I find out I was wrong too late
     I'm all alone
Alone in the world of broken hearts

I live in the world world of
     forgotten people
Who've loved and lost their hearts
     so many times
I'm here in a world world of
     forgotten people
Where every heart is aching just
     like mine

OPPOSITE Loretta with fans,
1960

"When They Ring Those Golden Bells"

RELEASE DATE 1963
ALBUM *Hymns*

There's a land beyond the river
That we call the sweet forever
And we only reach that shore by
     faith you see
Yes, I want to see my Jesus
Shake His hand and hear Him
     greet us
When they ring those golden bells
     for you and me.

Don't you hear the bells a ringing
Can't you hear the angels singing
This glory hallelujah jubilee
In that far-off great forever just
     beyond the shining river
When they ring those golden bells
     for you and me.

When our days have known their
     number
When in death we'll sweetly
     slumber
When the king commands the spirit
     to be free
There'll be no more stormy weather
We'll live peacefully together
When they ring those golden bells
     for you and me.

Don't you hear the bells a ringing
Can't you hear the angels singing
This glory hallelujah jubilee
In that far-off great forever just
     beyond the shining river
When they ring those golden bells
     for you and me . . .

"Where Were You"

RELEASE DATE 1964
ALBUM *Before I'm Over You*

Where were you when you left my
heart alone
And the nights you didn't bother to
come home
Now you say my love's grown cold I
guess it's true
But when loneliness sits in where
were you

Where were you when we lost the
love we had
When I wanted you and needed
you so bad
Now you're blaming me for things I
didn't do
All the nights I spent a crying where
were you

The lonely hours were just too
much for me
With only tears to keep me
company
That's what destroyed the love that
we once knew
Stop and think when it happened
where were you

The lonely hours were just too
much for me
With only tears to keep me
company
That's what destroyed the love that
we once knew
Stop and think when it happened
where were you

"It Just Looks That Way"

RELEASE DATE 1965
ALBUM *Songs from My Heart*

No I'm not crying it just looks that
way
He thinks his leaving me will drive
me mad silly boy he's the smallest
hurt I've had
These ain't tears I'm standing in it
rains today
No I'm not crying it just looks that
way
No I'm not crying it just looks that
way
I convince my heart I'm happy and
make believe everything I say
He thinks he left me lonesome and
hurtin' every day
Oh but I'm not crying it just looks
that way

No I'm not crying . . .
Oh but I'm not crying it just looks
that way

"When Lonely Hits Your Heart"

RELEASE DATE 1965
ALBUM *Songs from My Heart*

Here I am a doing things I said I'd
    never do
But that's before my baby said
    we're through
It was on that tragic day the hurtin'
    got its start
That's how it is when lonely hits
    your heart
I've become a fallen girl for the love
    of a man
The same old thing goes on and on
    it's more than I can stand
To him it just don't matter but it's
    tearing me apart
That's how it is when lonely hits
    your heart

I spent my nights a crying while he
    was running round
My heart was the first place lonely
    found
I don't think I'll forget him I can't
    begin to start
That's how it is when lonely hits
    your heart
I've become a fallen girl . . .

"Farther to Go"

RELEASE DATE 1965
ALBUM *Blue Kentucky Girl*

I've been up to the top of a
    heartbreak mountain
I've been down in the valley of the
    blues
I've been down the road of
    loneliness and back again
And I've got farther to go than I've
    been
I've been down in the dust of
    broken mem'ries
I've been up on the clouds of
    happiness
I've seen many a glass held high in
    the house of sin
And I've got farther to go than I've
    been
I've got farther to go I've got things
    to forget
I've got things I remember about
    you
I've been up when you told me that
    you love me
I went down when you told me we
    were through
Cried until my eyes would dry then I
    cried again
And I've got farther to go than I've
    been yes I've got farther to go
    than I've been

OPPOSITE Loretta, 1960,
publicity photo

Connie Francis

When I put my little band together out in the state of Washington, we would play in these tiny taverns all over the state and we would have to play for about four hours each night. People love to dance, so I learned all kinds of songs that I thought folks would like to hear but also dance to. Connie Francis was a big star back then and not just a pop star—everybody loved her. She was one of my husband Doolittle's favorite singers. He also thought she was "one good-looking woman," as he would say. I think he was just trying to make me mad. But I learned a couple of Connie's songs, as well, to sing in my sets. A few years ago someone from Washington, where we lived, sent me a tape of one of my old band rehearsals, and on that dad-gum tape was me trying to sing one of Connie's big hits called "Stupid Cupid." Lord, that was the funniest thang I've ever heard. Somehow, my daughter Patsy got a hold of that tape, and she came to me all excited, hollering, "Momma, I was listening to your old tape, and I heard this song you were singing called 'Stupid Cupid'…it's a hit!!" Poor thing, it broke her heart when I told her I didn't write it. But Patsy went and bought every Connie Francis record she could find. Yes, she is her daddy's daughter!

"Two Steps Forward"

RELEASE DATE 1965
ALBUM *Blue Kentucky Girl*

Well here you come and I know
what I'm gonna say
My mind's made up and I'm a
leavin' you today
Well I'm tired of askin' you where
you've been I'm tired of all this
mis'ry I'm in
Two steps forward and six steps
back again
Well my clothes're packed and I'm a
headin' for the door
Don't look for me back 'cause I
won't be back no more
Well I may think of you now and
then
But don't hold your breath 'cause I
don't know when
Two steps forward and six steps
back again
Two steps forward and six steps
back you think I didn't want to go
These tears in my eyes they're not
so real I'm just puttin' on a show
I'm leavin' this town and that's for
certain
Not much I ain't a cryin' not much I
ain't a hurtin'
Two steps forward and six steps
back again

Two steps forward and six steps
back . . .
Yeah two steps forward and six
steps back again

Everybody Wants to Go to Heaven

RELEASE DATE 1965
ALBUM *Hymns*

Everybody wants to go to heaven
but nobody wants to die

Once upon a time there lived a man
and his name was Hezekiah
He walked with God both day and
night but he didn't wanna die
He cried O Lord please let me live
death is close I know
God smiled down on Hezekiah and
gave him fifteen years to go

Everybody wants to go to heaven
but nobody wants to die
Lord I wanna go to heaven but I
don't wanna die
So I long for the day when I'll have
on Earth
Everybody wants to go to heaven
but nobody wants to die

When Jesus lived here on this Earth
He knew His father's plan
He knew that He must give His life
to save the soul of men
When Judas had betrayed Him his
father heard Him cry
He was brave until his death but He
didn't wanna die

Everybody wants to go to
heaven but nobody wants to die
Lord I wanna go to heaven but I
don't wanna die
So I long for the day when I'll have
on Earth

Everybody wants to go to heaven
but nobody wants to die

Everybody wants to go to heaven
but nobody wants to die

"Night Girl"

WRITTEN WITH Teddy Wilburn
RELEASE DATE 1965
ALBUM *Blue Kentucky Girl*

You say you'd like to be with me
tonight someplace where we can
hide from your world
But if you're ashamed to show me
up in daylight
Then I can't see why I should be
your night girl
I guess you think I'll be your poor
girl prize who'll never fit into your
social world
But if you're too good for me in
your own eyes
Then I can't see why I should be
your night girl
You were born into a wealthy
family I was born into a world of
poverty
So if you're too proud to have me in
your world
Then I can't see why I should be
your night girl

You were born into a wealthy
family . . .

OPPOSITE Mooney and
Loretta right after they
married, 1948

"Love's Been Here and Gone"

WRITTEN WITH Teddy Wilburn
RELEASE DATE 1965
ALBUM *Blue Kentucky Girl*

Love's been here and gone but the
mem'ry keeps holding on
Now I know how I'd be if I can live
through this love's been here and
gone
When there's love your heart is
strong but it weakens when love
goes wrong
Now I've known that power dealt
the parting hour love's been here
and gone
I've loved once but never again a
closed heart just won't let love in
Hopin' only to you oh what can I do
love's been here and gone

I've loved once but never again . . .

"The Third Man"

WRITTEN WITH Frances Irene Heighton,
Don Helms, and Teddy Wilburn
RELEASE DATE 1965
ALBUM *Hymns*

Last night I dreamed I took a walk
up Calvary's lonely hill
The things I saw with my own eyes
could not have been more real

I saw upon three crosses three men
in agony
Two cried out for mercy and the
third man looked at me

And oh the hurt in this man's eyes
  just broke my heart in two
It seemed that I could hear him say,
  I'm doing this for you

I knelt beneath the third man's
  cross and slowly bowed my head
I reached out and I touch his feet
  and it stained my hands with red
And when I heard him cryin'
  I raised my eyes to see
The blood spilled from the third
  man's side some of it spilled
  on me

The third man wore a crown of
  thorns spikes held him to the tree
And I heard him say oh God my God
  why hast Thou forsaken me
And there among a mighty crowd
  the ones who mocked him cried
If thou art King then save thyself
  and then the third man died

Suddenly I heard the thunder roll
  and saw lightning pierce the sky
The third man was still hanging
  there and I began to cry
I saw the boulders fall, and heard
  the breaking of the ground
Then, I awoke and though I
  dreamed, I touched my cheek and
  found

My eyes were wet where I had
  cried, a dream? I wish I knew
I still can hear the third man say,
  "I'm doing this for you."

"Where I Learned to Pray"

RELEASE DATE 1965
ALBUM *Hymns*

In our little one-room country
  school it's where I learned to pray
A church without a steeple that's
  where I learned to pray
Every Sunday morning about the
  hour of ten
The door would open to our school
  the preacher did walk in
He'd smile and say good morning
  how's everything today
We'd bow our heads and close our
  eyes and then he'd say let's pray
In our little one-room country
  school it's where I learned to pray
Our church that had no steeple is
  no longer there today
From Monday until Friday at school
  we'd learn and play
Then back at school on Sunday
  that's where I learned to pray

Our clothes were clean but faded
  sometimes our feet were bare
But no one noticed anything except
  the Lord was there
We'd come from all directions
  searching for the way
Harmonies at school on Sunday
  that's where I learned to pray
In our little one-room . . .

Ernest Tubb

My daddy saved enough money to buy an old radio, and every Saturday night he would turn it on so he could listen to the *Grand Ole Opry*. I tell you, that was living big to all of us. Mommy would gather all us kids and sometimes we would pop corn, dance, and sing along with all the Opry stars. My daddy loved Ernest Tubb. When it was Ernest's time to sing, Daddy would make everybody be quiet so he could hear him. So it was so special to me when I got to sing on the *Grand Ole Opry* for the first time. I was put on Ernest Tubb's part of the show and Ernest introduced me onstage. I know my daddy was smilin' down from heaven on that one. I loved Ernest so much that I named my son after him, only his name is Ernest Ray. Later, after I really got started recording my own records, me and Ernest Tubb got together and recorded two albums together. I wrote a song for us called "We're Not Kids Anymore." Singing that song I wrote and hearing Ernest Tubb doing one of my songs . . . I have to say, it was one of the greatest thrills of my life.

Loretta and Ernest Tubb, 1980

Loretta and Mooney the first time WSM played "Honky Tonk Girl"

"We're Not Kids Anymore"

RELEASE DATE 1965
ALBUM *Ernest Tubb and Loretta Lynn, Mr. and Mrs. Used to Be*

The man who recorded this song with me was a very special person to me. I looked up to him; he was one of my idols. The first time I walked onstage with him I could not believe that I was singing with the man I had listened to when I was a little girl. I used to cry when he sang "It's Been So Long Darling" and "Rainbow at Midnight." Mommy would threaten to turn the radio off if I didn't quit crying. That feeling of genuine love stayed the same from the first time I was onstage with him right up to the last time. One of my greatest pleasures is that he told me this was his favorite song that we ever recorded together. I really miss Ernest Tubb.

**We're not kids anymore
Not a little girl and boy
But we break each other's hearts
Like a child breaks a toy
We're a woman and a man
Watching love slip through our
    hands
Let's grow up, we're not kids
    anymore.**

**I go out of my way
To hurt you more every day
And you cry like your little heart
    will break
And every time you make me blue
I make a point to hurt you, too
And I wonder how much more our
    love can take**

**We're not kids anymore
Not a little girl and boy
But we break each other's hearts
Like a child breaks a toy
We're a woman and a man
Watching love slip through our
    hands
Let's grow up, we're not kids
    anymore.**

"Country Christmas"

RELEASE DATE 1966
ALBUM *Country Christmas*

Owen Bradley wanted to record a Christmas record. He had a bunch of songs picked out for me. Most were just good ol' standard Christmas songs like "Jingle Bells." He said that I should write a Christmas song. I just laughed and told him that where I came from, there wasn't much of a Christmas, we were too poor. I told him how we didn't have money for Christmas, but how Daddy would go cut us a cedar tree and Mommy and us kids would pop popcorn and thread it on a string to hang on the tree and how we would all sing songs together. Those memories got me thinkin', so one Christmas I went home and wrote "Country Christmas" that night and recorded it the next day.

Loretta with her producer, Owen Bradley, 1970s

Mommie pop the popcorn and we'll
   string it on the tree
Apple nuts and candy oh what a
   Christmas feel
Daddy play the organ and we'll all
   sing "Silent Night"
We'll have a good ole country
   Christmas alright

A good ole country Christmas that's
   what it's gonna be
With all the family gathered round
   our pretty Christmas tree
We'll open up our presents
   Christmas Eve about midnight
We'll have a good ole country
   Christmas alright

Aunt Annie Belle will be here Uncle
   Bill and their nine kids
We'll make pallets on the floor just
   like we always did
Grandma bake the pies and cakes
   oh what a pretty sight
We'll have a good ole country
   Christmas alright

A good ole country Christmas that's
   what it's gonna be
With all the family gathered round
   our pretty Christmas tree
We'll open up our presents
   Christmas Eve about midnight
We'll have a good ole country
   Christmas alright

"I Won't Decorate Your Christmas Tree"

WRITTEN WITH Bob Cummings, Barbara
Cummings, and Iva Cummings
RELEASE DATE 1966
ALBUM *Country Christmas*

Well I wrote to Santa just today I
   told him I don't plan to stay
'Cause you've been bad yes you've
   been treatin' me wrong
So listen to me here's Christmas
   cheers because you won't be
   seeing me here
I won't decorate your Christmas
   tree this year
You can stay out there to toast and
   cheer with all of your friends
Don't count on me a bein' here
   when you come back again
Your bags are burnt out and your
   fancy don't shine I just won't be a
   waitin' this time
I won't decorate your Christmas
   tree this year

Well I won't be here this Christmas
   Day I wouldn't get a present
   anyway
But have a good time and be
   concerned about me
I'm going back to my mom and dad
   they love me more than you ever
   had
I won't decorate your Christmas
   tree this year
You can stay out there . . .
No I won't decorate your Christmas
   tree this year

"To Heck with Ole Santa Claus"

RELEASE DATE 1966
ALBUM *Country Christmas*

"To Heck with Ole Santa Claus" is my favorite Christmas song that I've written. I'd tell Doo every year what I wanted him to get me for Christmas. Never anything big, just little things—this or that. He would never listen. He always would buy me something I didn't ask for. But I always loved whatever he gave me.

(To heck with ole Santa Claus)
Last year I hung my stocking by
   the chimney and ole Santa didn't
   bring me anything
Well I wrote a note and I told him
   what to bring me
But I didn't even hear his sleigh
   bells ring

So to heck with ole Santa Claus
When he goes dashin' through the
   snow I hope he falls
I'd like to hit him in his ho ho ho
   with a bunch of big snowballs
To heck with ole Santa Claus

This year I'll build a big fire in the
   fireplace I'll be like the little pig I
   read about
If that big bad wolf in red comes
   down my chimney
He's a gonna scorch his whiskers
   no doubt

So to heck with ole Santa Claus
When he goes dashin' through the
   snow I hope he falls
I'd like to hit him in his ho ho ho
   with a bunch of big snowballs
To heck with ole Santa Claus

Yeah to heck with ole Santa Claus

"It Won't Seem Like Christmas"

RELEASE DATE 1966
ALBUM *Country Christmas*

Everybody's busy decorating
   Christmas trees
And outside icicles hanging from
   the eaves
And the snowflakes are flyin' just as
   far as I can see
But it won't seem like Christmas
   to me
No it won't seem like Christmas
   you'll be there and I'll be here
So I'll decorate a heartache with my
   tears
So have a merry merry Christmas
   wherever you may be
Oh but it won't seem like Christmas
   to me

No it won't seem like Christmas
   what's Christmas without you
I'll be lonely but my darling I'll be
   true
So have a merry merry
   Christmas . . .
No it won't seem like Christmas
   to me

I played on Loretta Lynn's first Decca recording session. When it was over, I went into the control room and said to my brother, Owen Bradley, "Whatever is in that woman's heart comes right out her mouth." Owen said, "I know, that's why I signed her. I thought she was sincere."

Obviously we were both right!!

HAROLD BRADLEY

"Dear Uncle Sam"

RELEASE DATE 1966
ALBUM *I Like 'Em Country*

When I wrote this song in the sixties, all you could hear about on the radio was the Vietnam War. My husband and I were driving one afternoon, and we were listening to one of those news breaks on the radio. He looked over at me and said, "Loretta, why don't you write a song about the war?"

I said, "Doo, I don't know anything good about war, so I really don't know what there is good to write about it."

He said, "What's wrong with writing to Uncle Sam?"

And I realized he's the man that all the mothers ought to write to. I wrote the song and recorded it about three weeks later with Boots Randolph playing "Taps." They put him in the bathroom of the studio with the door open because the sound was not sounding just right in the studio. It's always been one of my favorite songs to sing out on the road at my live show. Whenever I get a request to sing it, I give the credit for this song to the man I love: my husband.

**Dear Uncle Sam, I know you're a
  busy man
And tonight I write to you through
  tears with a trembling hand
My darling answered when he got
  that call from you
You said you really need him but
  you don't need him like I do
Don't misunderstand I know he's
  fighting for our land
I really love my country but I also
  love my man
He proudly wears the colors of the
  old red white and blue
While I wear a heartache since he
  left me for you**

**Dear Uncle Sam, I just got your
  telegram
And I can't believe that this is me
  shaking like I am
For it said I'm sorry to inform you**

"Darkest Day"

RELEASE DATE 1966
ALBUM *You Ain't Woman Enough*

Darlin' when you told me you were
    leavin' I thought that you were
    only foolin' me
But here I am to face old blue
    tomorrow with a broken heart
    that's filled with misery
It seems that my world is through
    an end
Just dreamin' of things that might
    have been
Oh why don't that ole sun shine
    bright
Today's the darkest day of my life

Oh how I wish that old saying is
    true
It's always the darkest just before
    dawn
Then I'll know soon I'm gonna see
    the sun-shine
I just can't take this darkness on
    and on

It seems that my world is through
    an end
Just dreamin' of things that might
    have been
Oh why don't that ole sun shine
    bright today's the darkest day of
    my life

"God Gave Me a Heart to Forgive"

WRITTEN WITH Bob Cummings and
Barbara Cummings
RELEASE DATE 1966
ALBUM *You Ain't Woman Enough*

It's midnight now and I'm still all
    alone,
It's always late each night when
    you come home.
I stay and take each heartache that
    you give,
'Cause God gave me a heart to
    forgive.

You hurt me as much as you can,
Then you tell me that you're just
    weak like any other man.
Still you're the only reason that I
    live,
And God gave me a heart to
    forgive.

Guess I could call these tears my
    closest friends,
They stay with me 'til you come
    home again.
You've brought me every misery
    that there is,
But God gave me a heart to forgive.

You hurt me as much as you can,
Then you tell me that you're just
    weak like any other man.
Still you're the only reason that I
    live,
And God gave me a heart to
    forgive.

"Keep Your Change"

RELEASE DATE 1966
ALBUM *You Ain't Woman Enough*

You need a change of scenery that's
all I ever heard
And when you left and you said
goodbye I never said a word
You're back but I don't want you
back to you that might seem
strange
But I ain't buyin' what she bought
so honey keep your change
Yeah honey keep your change and
the trouble that she brings
You've worked real hard for what
you got so honey keep your
change

What happened to the scenery that
looked so good to you
Did you get tired of the change you
made or did she get tired of you
You're like a travelin' salesman and
I hear they're all the same
So travel right on back to her yeah
honey keep your change
Yeah honey keep your change . . .
Yeah honey keep your change . . .
Yeah honey keep your change yeah
honey keep your change

"Man I Hardly Know"

RELEASE DATE 1966
ALBUM *You Ain't Woman Enough*

In a booth back in a corner where
the lights are way down low
In the arms of a man I hardly know

I let the devil take over this heart of
mine
When I lost your love well I almost
lost my mind
I never thought I'd ever fall this low
but here I am with a man I hardly
know
In a booth back in a corner . . .

I do the things a proper lady
wouldn't do
And it all started that first night
when I lost you
To see me now you wouldn't know
me I'm changed so
'Cause here I am with a man I
hardly know
In a booth back in a corner . . .

STEREO

DECCA RECORDS

I LIKE 'EM
COUNTRY

LORETTA
LYNN

INCLUDING:
JEALOUS HEART
CRY CRY CRY
YOUR CHEATIN' HEART
IF TEARDROPS WERE PENNIES
ITS BEEN SO LONG, DARLING

Printed in U.S.A.

"You Ain't Woman Enough"

RELEASE DATE 1966
ALBUM *You Ain't Woman Enough*

I gave birth to this song, and I felt every little bit of pain in these lyrics. You know a woman likes to feel sure of a man—but there are times when things just don't play out that way. Do I have to say more about that? I think in every marriage, at one time or the other, a woman worries about the *other* woman—who may or may not exist. In my case, in *this* case, I had to be sure. Over the years, a lot of my fans have become close friends, and we tell each other all our problems. One night, at one of my live shows, me and a girlfriend were talking. She told me her husband, who was there with her, was running around on her. She was crying because when she came through the door to get in to the show, she saw the other woman was also there. I said, "We will fix that old gal." That night I sang "You Ain't Woman Enough" and dedicated it to her. Girlfriends gotta stick together.

You've come to tell me something
   you say I ought to know
That he don't love me anymore and
   I'll have to let him go
You say you're gonna take him oh
   but I don't think you can
'Cause you ain't woman enough to
   take my man

Women like you they're a dime a
   dozen you can buy 'em anywhere
For you to get to him I'd have to
   move over and I'm gonna stand
   right here
It'll be over my dead body so get
   out while you can
'Cause you ain't woman enough to
   take my man

Sometimes a man caught lookin' at
   things that he don't need
He took a second look at you but
   he's in love with me
Well I don't know where that leaves
   you oh but I know where I stand
And you ain't woman enough to
   take my man

Women like you they're a dime . . .
No you ain't woman enough to
   take my man

Songwriting

Every marriage has problems ... but everybody ain't meant to be a song-writer. Poor Doolittle couldn't get away with nothin'. If he did anything, I would write a song about it and the world would know. But Doo never got mad at me, I don't think. He never would say if he did. I'd play him a song, and I know he knew it was about him.

He would just say, "That's a good one, honey."

I believe that me being able to write about things was my way of dealing with my problems. Just writing them down on a page made me feel better. And helped me understand what was happening in my life.

Mooney in Washington
State, 1950s

"Look Who's Lonely"

RELEASE DATE 1966
ALBUM *Wilburn Brothers Album*

Well how many times have you
    waved bye bye
And left me at home just to sit and
    cry?
Now look who's lonely look who's
    blue
You didn't think you could ever lose
Now look who's wearin' my old
    shoes
Yeah look who's lonely look who's
    blue

You're wantin' me to take you back
    you're beggin' me to try
You can't look me in the eye when
    you say you've changed
'Cause it's just another lie
Stop where you are 'cause you can't
    come in
You ain't a gonna get in my heart
    again
Now look who's lonely look who's
    blue!

You're down on your knees outside
    my door
But I haven't heard enough I wanna
    hear some more
Now look who's lonely look who's
    blue
Now that all the neighbors are
    laughin' at you
I guess you know I think it kinda
    funny too
Yeah look who's lonely look who's
    blue

You're wantin' me to take you back
    you're beggin' me to try
You can't look me in the eye when
    you say you've changed
'Cause it's just another lie
Stop where you are 'cause you can't
    come in
You ain't a gonna get in my heart
    again
Now look who's lonely look who's
    blue!

Yeah look who's lonely look who's
    blue.

Peggy Sue

There was eight kids in my family. Back then, it seems like folks just had bigger families. When my mommy got pregnant with my little sister Peggy Sue, she already had five kids. Back then it was different. Everybody helped out doing whatever our mommy and daddy said. Cleaning, cooking, helping watch the little kids. Anything.

When Mommy had Peggy Sue, she told me it was my job to help with the new baby. I thought she was giv-ing her to me! And I loved Peggy Sue so much. I would rock her, dress her, bathe her. Like I said, I thought she was mine. So when Doo and I got married, I was packing up what little clothes I had to leave, and I started packing Peggy Sue's, too. My mommy came in the room and said, "Loretty, what are you packing Peggy Sue's clothes for?"

I said, "I am taking her with me."

Mommy told me, "You can't take Peggy Sue!"

Loretta and daughter Betty Sue, 1950s

I said, "Why, Mommy? You gave her to me!"

I cried more having to leave Peggy Sue behind than because I was leaving period. She and I have always been real close. In the early sixties I was living in Nashville and recording. I had a few big records out and was really getting a lot of attention. People were saying I was one of the top female singers. Doo and I went to Indiana to visit one time, and my mommy said, "Loretty, have you heard Peggy Sue sing?" I hadn't but come to find out Peggy Sue was a really good singer and songwriter. She moved to Nashville, and we started working together. We sang our songs. Peggy Sue had the great idea for "Don't Come Home a Drinkin'." She had the song already started, and then we finished it up, and it was a big hit for me. I finally talked Owen Bradley into recording Peggy Sue on her own, and we got her signed to Decca as well. I wrote a song called "I'm Dynamite" for Peggy Sue, and it was a number one hit for her. She sang background vocals and traveled with me a lot out on the road. Then, in the mid-seventies, we started working with Crystal Gayle, who was just getting started on her own career. We are still real close and talk to each other a lot. Sometimes when Crystal ain't working, Peggy will hop on the bus with me and sing and tell jokes in my shows. The crowd just loves her. I don't think I could have made it this long on the road without my family being around. Peggy Sue is still writing songs . . . great ones. I keep telling her and Crystal we are going to record together. We haven't ever got to do that yet. I am so glad my brother and sisters got to be in the music business with me. And I owe a big thanks to Peggy Sue for coming up with "Don't Come Home a Drinkin'." I love her.

Don't Come Home a Drinkin' (With Lovin' on Your Mind)

WRITTEN WITH Peggy Sue Wells
RELEASE DATE 1967
ALBUM *Don't Come Home a Drinkin'*

This song started my first little sister, Peggy Sue, in country music. I had just got started myself and was in Indiana doing two or three shows. Naturally, I was spending the night with Mommy. Peggy showed me a song she was writing. She was married and had a little girl and was starting to find out that no matter how good life is, it does have its ups and downs. She was trying to do the same thing that I did when I started—sing and write songs and start a whole life in music—and was having the same problems I did. I looked at what she had on paper, and I kind of knew what she was trying to say. It's like when there's twins, the old saying is, "What one can't think of, the other one can." I've always had this feeling with Peggy that I am kind of inside her head. Maybe it's because she means so much to me. We can look at each other and know what the other is thinking. Sometimes it's not too good to be like that, but when the song was finished, we both thought it was great so I took it to Sure-Fire Music Co., the company I wrote for. The Wilburn Brothers, who owned the company, thought it was great. A lot of people must have felt like that, 'cause it sure was a hit.

Well you thought I'd be waitin' up
  when you came home last night
You'd been out with all the boys
  and you ended up half tight
But liquor and love that just don't
  mix leave a bottle or me behind
And don't come home a drinkin'
  with lovin' on your mind
No don't come home a drinkin'
  with lovin' on your mind
Just stay out there on the town and
  see what you can find
'Cause if you want that kind of love
  well you don't need none of mine
So don't come home a drinkin' with
  lovin' on your mind

You never take me anywhere
  because you're always gone
Many a night I've laid awake and
  cried dear all alone
And you come in a kissin' on me it
  happens every time
No don't come home a drinkin'
  with lovin' on your mind
No don't come home a drinkin' . . .
No don't come home a drinkin'
  with lovin' on your mind

"Get What'cha Got and Go"

WRITTEN WITH Ron Williams and Leona Williams
RELEASE DATE 1967
ALBUM *Don't Come Home a Drinkin'*

Purty Boy Charlie's the name that
    you've been given,
And you act like the whole wide
    world owes you a livin',
You tell me you can get any girl you
    know,
You say you got what it takes, to
    me you're just a heartache.
So get what'cha got and go.

You think you're the greatest thing
    in this old town,
Ol' number one with everyone, no
    one can put you down.
Every night you go downtown
    where the Go-Gos go,
Well, ya think you're so hot and ya
    tell me you're not,
So get what'cha got and go.

You better wipe that sneaky smile
    right off your face
'Fore I just must knock it off, and
    put you in your place.
Just like the wild, wild wind, all you
    do is blow.
You say I'm holdin' you back
Well, baby, I'll help you pack.
So, get what'cha got and go.

"I Got Caught"

RELEASE DATE 1967
ALBUM *Don't Come Home a Drinkin'*

You're standin' there a sayin' I'm no
    good and I'm so ashamed I'd die
    if I could
But you're no better than I am or
    have you given this one thought
The only thing that's different I got
    caught
Of all the nights you left me all
    alone and the only arms close to
    me was my own
And now you're blamin' me but it's
    not all my fault
The only thing that's different I got
    caught

Yeah I got caught but honey you're
    a pro
There's not a thing about cheatin'
    you don't know
That same old line you sell is the
    same old line I bought
The things you've got away with I
    got caught

Yeah I got caught but honey you're
    a pro
There's not a thing about cheatin'
    you don't know
That same old line you sell is the
    same old line I bought
The things you've got away with I
    got caught

Yeah the things you've got away
    with I got caught

"Bartender"

WRITTEN WITH Maggie Vaughn
RELEASE DATE 1967
ALBUM *Ernest Tubb and Loretta Lynn, Singin' Again*

Please listen to me bartender I've
    got something on my mind
I think I might feel better after one
    more glass of wine
I'm payin' for a broken heart the
    price of love is high
With nothing left to live for what's
    there to do but die
(I know your story honey they're all
    the same you see
Why I knew the minute that you
    walked in you want to talk to me
But I've learned what you don't
    read in books from words that
    cost this bar
I've seen them come and I've seen
    them drink
Till they don't even know who they
    are
Now I don't believe that honky
    tonk is a place for a girl like you
I might be wrong but you don't
    look right sittin' there on that bar
    stool
It's not too late so stop and think
    before all of your pride is gone
You can end up like all the rest with
    a barroom for your home)
I know you're right bartender good
    night I'm going home

"Let's Stop Right Where We Are"

RELEASE DATE 1967
ALBUM *Ernest Tubb and Loretta Lynn, Singin' Again*

I know you've had a change of
    heart the way you're on the range
But the love for you that's in my
    heart is something you can't
    change
When you get your field of green
    green grass stay home and you'll
    find clover
Let's stop right where we are and
    start all over
Let's stop right where we are and
    start all over
Let's both admit that we've been
    wrong cry on each other's
    shoulder
Let's straighten up and save our
    love before we lose each other
Let's stop right where we are and
    start all over

You don't love on me anymore the
    way you used to do
So I went out looking for the love I
    failed to get from you
I'd make believe that it was you the
    nights when I would hold her
Let's stop right where we are and
    start all over
Let's stop right where we are . . .
Let's stop right where we are and
    start all over

Loretta on tour, 1960s

"Bargain Basement Dress"

RELEASE DATE 1967
ALBUM *Singin' with Feelin'*

Well on a Friday night you draw
   your pay and you take in the
   town
You leave me at home just to lose
   my mind while you're out messin'
   around
But it's four in the morning and you
   stagger in and you sure look a
   mess
With a smile on your face and
   outstretched arms and a bargain
   basement dress

I wouldn't wear that dress to a
   dogfight if the fight was free
And a bargain basement dress
   ain't enough to get your arms
   around me

Well they say when a man works
   hard all week he deserves to play
   or rest
Well honey that ain't right so get
   outta my sight with that bargain
   basement dress

I wouldn't wear that dress to a
   dogfight if the fight was free
And a bargain basement dress
   ain't enough to get your arms
   around me
Now I took all I'm gonna take and
   I'm a leavin' you the rest
Tell you what I'll do I'll just leave
   you that bargain basement dress
Tell you what I'll do I'll just leave
   you that old bargain basement
   dress

"I'll Sure Come a Long Way Down"

WRITTEN WITH Maggie Vaughn
RELEASE DATE 1967
ALBUM *Singin' with Feelin'*

Think I'll dye my hair blond today,
  to change my homey touch.
Might even learn a joke to tell that
  makes my pale face blush.
I'll change the high-neck dress
  I wear to a low-cut dress I've
  found.
To come up to what you're wantin'
  I'll sure come a long way down.

I'll put on my heavy makeup, so the
  real me won't show through
I'll be the things I hate the most, if I
  can be with you.
I'll come to the dark and dirty
  streets, in the roughest part of
  town.
To come up to what you're wantin',
  I'll sure come a long way down.

I'll wear my lipstick much too red,
  and a dress that fits too tight.
I'll be the kind of girl you want to fit
  into your life.
I'll give up everything that's good,
  be chained to the things you're
  bound,
To come up to what you're wanting,
  I'll sure come a long way down.

I'll put on my heavy makeup, so the
  real me won't show through
I'll be the things I hate the most, if I
  can be with you.

I'll come to the dark and dirty
  streets, in the roughest part of
  town.
To come up to what you're wantin',
  I'll sure come a long way down.

"Slowly Killing Me"

RELEASE DATE 1967
ALBUM *Singin' with Feelin'*

Oh I can't live without you and I'm
  barely livin' with you
I can't get her off your mind and I
  can't set you free
When you look at one another your
  look tells me you love her
And that's the part that's slowly
  killing me
Oh what's this other woman done
  to you she can't ever love you like
  I do
Cry tears enough to drown me
  heartache's closing in around me
And that's the part that's slowly
  killing me

Oh what's this other woman done
  to you why she can't ever love
  you like I do
I'd die the night you leave me I cry
  but you don't see me
And that's the part that's slowly
  killing me
Yes that's the part that's slowly
  killing me

"I Come Home a Drinkin' (to a Worn-Out Wife Like You)"

WRITTEN WITH Teddy Wilburn and Peggy Sue Wells
RELEASE DATE 1967
Released by Jay Lee Webb

"Don't Come Home a Drinkin'" was a number one hit for me, and I was trying to get my brother on the same record label I was on. Owen Bradley was waiting until we found a hit song, so I said to Teddy, "Let's write an answer to 'Don't Come Home a Drinkin'.'" So we grabbed an old shoe box, which was the first thing in sight, and he and I wrote "I Come Home a Drinkin' (to a Worn-Out Wife Like You)" and it was a number one record for my brother. We'd always called him Jack, ever since he was a baby, even though that wasn't his real name. I don't even remember why we did that, but Teddy just accepted it. We recorded him under the name of Jack Webb. Jack Webb, the star of the TV show *Dragnet,* was also under contract with Universal, which Decca Records owned at the time, and Jack Webb of *Dragnet* made us change Jack's stage name. We changed it to Jay Lee Webb.

I knew you'd be sleeping when I got
home last night
All you ever want to do is eat and
sleep and fight
You say you're always all worn out
from the work you have to do
So I come home a' drinkin' to a
worn-out wife like you.

Chorus:
Yes I come home a' drinkin' to a
worn-out wife like you
Seems like you never want to do
the things I like to do
Each time I try to hold you, you're
asleep before I do
So I come home a' drinkin' to a
worn-out wife like you

I never take you anywhere, 'cause
you're too tired to go
You say it's all that you can do to
wash and cook and sew
When you're too pooped to kiss
me, well, the bottle will have
to do
Then, I come home a' drinkin' to a
worn-out wife like you.

Jay Lee

Doo and I were married only about seven months. When we moved all the way from Kentucky to the state of Washington, to me it seemed like the other side of the world. Doo's family had lived in Washington on and off most of Doo's life, and he really loved it there. Leaving Butcher Holler was hard for me. I did not want to leave my mommy and daddy and family. But I was Doo's wife, and I was pregnant with our first baby. We moved to a town called Bellingham and lived on a farm owned by two brothers, Clyde and Bob Green. Doo got a job as a logger right away 'cause he knew how to drive a bulldozer and big trucks. I cooked and cleaned for the Greens, and in exchange they let us live in an old house they had there on their farm. It wasn't too long after we moved that my little brother Jack (Jay Lee) and me started singing and playing together. We played with lots of musicians and whatever band or players they had in the taverns. We

Loretta and Mooney's home in Hurricane Mills, Tennessee

would just get up and do a song or two. Later I put together my first band. We were called the Trail Blazers. I sang and played bar code rhythm, and Jack played lead guitar.

Jack and his wife, Sherrly, me and Doo, we were all real close. When we moved to Nashville, it wasn't long before Jack and Sherrly moved, too. Once I got my foot in the door and started recording a couple of records on Decca, I started helping Jack get himself a record deal with Decca. He was such a great singer. When we were trying to get him signed to his deal, the record company told us we would have to change his name. There was already a TV star named Jack Webb. So we called him Jay Lee from then on out. Jay Lee was like the rest of us Webbs . . . small. He wasn't but about five feet six inches. But, boy, he

could sure sing and play that guitar. He was the kind of person everybody loved. Always happy and friendly—never met a stranger 'cause everyone was his friend. When we finally got Jay Lee his record contract, I started writing songs for him to record. We wrote a few songs together, too. Jay Lee and I wrote an answer to my song "Don't Come Home a Drinkin'." It was called "I Come Home a Drinkin' (to a Worn-Out Wife Like You)." It was the funniest dang song you ever heard.

Jay Lee had a couple of pretty big records himself. I was so proud of him. Sometimes the Wilburns would have him come on and sing on their TV show. I always loved having him around. Later Jay Lee went to work for my little sister Crystal Gayle. He did that up until he got sick with cancer. He died in 1997. I miss him every day.

"Fist City"

RELEASE DATE 1968
ALBUM *Fist City*

I wrote this right after I bought the little town of Hurricane Mills, Tennessee. The way this song came about was my kids would come in and say, "Mommy, that old girl school-bus driver tells us that she's in love with Daddy and that she's going to take him away from us." Since I walked to our little one-room schoolhouse, I thought it was a joke when they said a woman was driving the school bus, because I didn't think women drove buses. It wasn't long after that I found out she really was spreading the news around town that she was in love with my husband. I knew he was no saint, but after seeing her I knew he had more class than that. Me and her and Doo met in our yard one day when I came in off tour, and they both said nothing was going on, and they both denied what was being said. But let's just put it this way: she didn't stay very long because she knew I was standing my ground. And since Hurricane Mills belongs to me, she knew she better detour 'round my town. And that's what she did.

You've been makin' your brags
   around town that you've been a
   lovin' my man
But the man I love when he picks
   up trash he puts it in a garbage
   can
And that's what you look like to me
   and what I see is a pity
You'd better close your face and
   stay out of my way
If you don't wanna go to Fist City

If you don't wanna go to Fist City
   you better detour round my town
'Cause I'll grab you by the hair of
   the head and I'll lift you off the
   ground
I'm not sayin' my baby is a saint
   'cause he ain't
And that he won't cat around with
   a kitty
I'm here to tell you gal to lay off of
   my man if you don't wanna go to
   Fist City

The front gates of Loretta and Mooney's home

Come on and tell me what you told
    my friends if you think you're
    brave enough
And I'll show you what a real
    woman is since you think you're
    hot stuff
You'll bite off more than you can
    chew if you get too cute or witty
You better move your feet if you
    don't wanna eat a meal that's
    Fist City
If you don't wanna go to Fist City
    you better detour round my town
'Cause I'll grab you by the hair of
    the head and I'll lift you off the
    ground
I'm not sayin' my baby is a saint
    'cause he ain't
And that he won't cat around with
    a kitty
I'm here to tell you gal to lay off of
    my man if you don't wanna go to
    Fist City

I'm here to tell you gal to lay off of
    my man if you don't wanna go to
    Fist City

"I'm Shootin' for Tomorrow"

RELEASE DATE 1968
ALBUM *Fist City*

It's a breakin' day and here you
    come with eyes as red as fire!
You tell me that you've done
    nothin' and you don't know how
    right you are
With the little home chores you
    used to do and they've all gone
    to pot
So I'm a shootin' for tomorrow
    'cause today's already shot
I'm a shootin' for tomorrow 'cause
    today's already shot
After all I'm gonna take and honey
    that's a lot
Well you used to think you's the
    only man but I found out you're
    not
So I'm a shootin' for tomorrow
    'cause today's already shot

I used to keep the home from
    burnin' but I let 'em all go out
So don't hand me that—
Now this old house is a gettin'
    cold and I'm a goin' where the
    climate's hot
So I'm a shootin' for tomorrow
    'cause today's already shot
I'm a shootin' for tomorrow . . .
I'm a shootin' for tomorrow 'cause
    today's already shot

"What Kind of Girl Do You Think I Am"

WRITTEN WITH Teddy Wilburn
RELEASE DATE 1968
ALBUM *Fist City*

Teddy Wilburn and I were on tour when we wrote this song. He and I did a lot of writing together, and I don't know which one of us thought of the idea. We just started writing. We never thought that a DJ would think, just by the title, that it might be bad, but a few stations banned it without even listening to it. Happily, the ones who played it made it number one. The story I would like to tell about this song is I was doing a show somewhere in Illinois and a preacher came backstage with the record for me to sign for his fifteen-year-old daughter. He hugged me and told me he loved me for writing the song, that it was one of the greatest messages that anybody could give a young girl who was just starting to

Loretta, 1970s

49

think about dating. After this happened, I really started to think about the effect my songs could have on people. I realized my songs could do more than make people happy or sad, they can make people think. Songs can make people change the things they do. I passed this song around to my own daughters, and I know a *lot* of daughters that it helped. All I have to say is: any young girl that has a problem with a boy that she goes with should be able to say to him, without any problem, "What kind of girl do you think I am?"

You want me to prove my love for
   you
I'm surprised that's the way you're
   askin' me to
You've known me so long I can't
   understand what kind of a girl do
   you think I am
What kind of a girl do you want for
   a wife
Do you want a girl who knows that
   much about life
Well if that's what you want take
   me out of your plans
What kind of a girl do you think
   I am

What kind of a girl would do
   the things you're askin' me to
   without wedding rings
Is it what you must do to prove
   you're a man what kind of a girl
   do you think I am
What kind of a girl . . .

"You Didn't Like My Lovin' "

WRITTEN WITH Red Hayes and
Doyle Wilburn
RELEASE DATE 1968
ALBUM *Fist City*

Don't you think it's a little too late
   to show those tears
Just look out the way you're treatin'
   me all these years
I'm a full-grown woman but you're
   treatin' me like a kid
You didn't like my lovin' so I found
   someone that did
You didn't like my lovin' so I found
   someone that did
And the one I found really made me
   flip my lid
After all that past I'm learnin' to
   live at last
You didn't like my lovin' so I found
   someone that did

Far as I'm concerned you can turn
   and walk out that door
'Cause the way we'd made it don't
   make it with me no more
Where your head used to lay there's
   another head there instead
You didn't like my lovin' so I found
   someone that did
You didn't like my lovin' . . .
You didn't like my lovin' so I found
   someone that did

"I'm a Gettin' Ready to Go"

RELEASE DATE 1968
ALBUM *Who Says God Is Dead?*

I get down on my knees every day
and I pray
These tears I'm a cryin' are tears of
joy 'cause it wash my sins away
I'm a livin' for the Lord and I want
everybody to know
This old world's just my dressin'
room and I'm a gettin' ready
to go
Yeah I'm a gettin' ready to go to a
place called heaven
I'm gonna praise my Saviour's name
every day that I'm livin'
Glory hallelujah I'm not ashamed
to let the salvation show
This old world's just my dressin'
room and I'm a gettin' ready
to go

I'm gonna walk in there with Jesus
and my God
I wanna know everything's a gonna
be alright when they lay me
under to sod
When He gathers His sheep I
wanna be as white as snow
This old world's just my dressin'
room and I'm a gettin' ready
to go
Yeah I'm a gettin' ready to go . . .
This old world's just my dressin'
room and I'm a gettin' ready
to go

"Mama Why?"

RELEASE DATE 1968
ALBUM *Who Says God Is Dead?*

(Oh Mama why did God take my
daddy 'cause I'd been good just
like he said to be
I heard Daddy pray dear Lord don't
take me from them
Oh Mama why did God take him
from me)

Come here son you've asked Mama
somethin' that's even hard for me
to understand
But there's one thing I do know
Daddy wouldn't wanna see those
tears in the eyes of his big man
So stop cryin' now and listen real
careful to every word that Mama
has to say
You see son God picks the sweetest
most beautiful flowers that grow
And he makes them the brightest
shiniest stars that glow

Now Daddy talked with the Lord
everyday and Daddy and God'll
be real close
So let's just say it seems that God
takes the ones he loves the most

(Oh Mama why did God take my
daddy)
Son you haven't heard a word that
Mama said

So come on now let's say your
prayers and Mama tuck you in
bed

And we mustn't question God
'cause he already has everything
planned
And honey Daddy can't ever come
back to us but we can go to him

(Oh Mama why did God take my
Daddy)

"Who Says God Is Dead?"

RELEASE DATE 1968
ALBUM *Who Says God Is Dead?*

At the time I wrote this song there was lots of talk about God being dead. I don't know why, 'cause even if you were out of your mind, how could you say God is dead? It was in the late sixties when it seemed like everyone in the whole world was doing their thing. I thought, "How sick can one get? 'Cause all I can say is the God I worship is very much alive." Who says God is dead? Not me!

(Who says God is dead who says
God is dead)
Who says God is dead I'm a talkin'
to Him now
Who says God is dead He's with us
all right now
He knows every move that you
make He knows every time you
make a mistake
The rumor has been spread who
says God is dead

Who says God is dead that's
stoopin' mighty low
I like to meet 'em face to face and
tell 'em it's not so
I've got my Savior by the hand He's
leadin' me to the Promised Land
No I'm not out of my head who says
God is dead

Who says God is dead He's a
watchin' you right now
Who says God is dead He's a
reachin' for you now
If I were you I'd kneel and pray
'cause we're not promised one
more day
Remember blood was shed who
says God is dead

Who says God is dead
that's stoopin' mighty low
I like to meet 'em face to face and
tell 'em it's not so
I've got my Savior by the hand and
He's leadin' me to the Promised
Land
No I'm not out of my head, who
says God is dead
Who says God is dead
Who says God is dead
Who says God is dead

"Gonna Pack My Troubles"

RELEASE DATE 1968
ALBUM *Here's Loretta Lynn*

I'm gonna pack my troubles in a
big suitcase and dump 'em in the
deep blue sea

Come all you lovers from misery
  lane and tag along with me
Well I'm tired of livin' this kind of
  life, wantin' things that just
  can't be
I'm gonna pack my troubles in a
  big suitcase and dump 'em in the
  deep blue sea

But that old sun, it'll start to shine
  and I won't be blue no more
Well, then I'll find myself a brand-
  new love, that's what I'm longin'
  for
Well, the loves I've had, they've
  made me sad, left my heart
  swingin' from a tree
I'm gonna pack my troubles in a
  big suitcase and dump 'em in the
  deep blue sea

Well that old sun, it'll start to shine
  and I won't be blue no more
Well, then I'll find myself a brand
  new love, that's what I'm longin'
  for
Well, the loves I've had, they've
  made me sad, left my heart
  swingin' from a tree
I'm gonna pack my troubles in a
  big suitcase and dump 'em in the
  deep blue sea

And dump them in the deep blue
  sea

"Heartache Meet Mr. Blues"

RELEASE DATE 1968
ALBUM *Here's Loretta Lynn*

Well here I am with my head
  bowed low, my tears they're
  rolling down.
My baby's with somebody new, in a
  honky tonk in town.

Hello, Mister Lonesome, did you
  bring any news?
Oh come on in, Mister Heartache,
  and meet old Mister Blues.

When my baby left this morning,
  said he wouldn't be home no
  more
I can still hear the echo of him
  slamming my back door.

Hello, Mister Lonesome, did you
  bring any news?
Oh come on in, Mister Heartache,
  and meet old Mister Blues.

"Stop"

RELEASE DATE 1968
ALBUM *Here's Loretta Lynn*

Stop, you're fooling me
Stop, and let me be
I can't understand a love that's
  secondhand,
When it's untrue and just like
  drifting sand.

Stop, danger's in sight, oh
Stop, it's just not right

To break a heart like mine and then
  leave me behind, oh please
Stop 'cause you know I'm not your
  kind.

Why do you want to do me this a
  way,
When you have yourself a new girl
  every day?

Oh please stop, danger's ahead. Oh,
Stop, this life you've led.
Someday you will see just what
  you've done to me,
You'll be glad to say that you're
  sorry.

"New Rainbow"

RELEASE DATE 1968
ALBUM *Here's Loretta Lynn*

There's a new rainbow in the sky,
I can see the starlight in the sky
Those love beams shine on Cupid's
  bow,
I'm in love with you, I know.

I've been searching all around to
  find someone like you
And now I'm going to settle down,
  I've found someone that's true.
That rainbow will never fade away
For I know our love is here to stay.

You put a rainbow in my heart
I know you won't tear it apart
And if you say you love me, too
Then our dreams will all come true.

I've been searching all around to
  find someone like you
And now I'm going to settle down,
  I've found someone that's true.
That rainbow will never fade away
For I know our love is here to stay.

"Blue Steel"

RELEASE DATE 1968
ALBUM *Here's Loretta Lynn*

Well, I was feelin' mighty
  lonesome, through my tears I
  could hardly see.
When the flashing lights from a
  honky tonk were inviting me.
Well I sit down at my table with my
  head in my hand,
And I watched him dance so close
  to her to the honky tonk band.

It was then I heard the fiddle play,
  the guitar played it too.
And that old steel guitar, it cried
  and kept on playin' the blues.

Well, I ordered up just one more
  drink, I thought would ease my
  mind
But I found out it didn't help, for a
  love-sick heart that's blind.
Old memories keep comin' back,
  old memories of you
And of the time that you once said,
  that no one else would do.

It was then I heard the fiddle play,
  the guitar played it too.
And that old steel guitar, it cried
  and kept on playin' the blues.

"My Angel Mother"

RELEASE DATE 1968
ALBUM *Here's Loretta Lynn*

I'll never forget the day I wrote "My Angel Mother." It was the third song I had ever written. I walked into my bedroom, and as I passed the mirror, for just an instant, I thought it was my mother. I looked so much like her that I even said, "Mommy." Then I realized that Mommy was three thousand miles away. I never felt that my mother was any less than an angel. Every Mother's Day I sung this song to Mommy, and since Mommy's gone I still sing it, just knowing she's listening.

I'm writing this song about a girl
   that I know
She's just as pure as all silver and
   gold
I might search this world over, but
   I'd never find

No one to take the place of this
   mother of mine

Mother, That's the sweetest name
   of them all
You're an Angel on Earth and to me
   you are worth
More than anything else in the
   world

I love you more day by day and I
   could never repay
All the things that you've done
   for me
Your heart is filled with joyous
   times
And your eyes how they shine
That's the story of this Mother of
   mine.

Mother, That's the sweetest name
   of them all
You're an Angel on Earth and to me
   you are worth
More than mountains of silver and
   gold

Ted and Clara Webb,
Loretta's mom and dad,
on their wedding day

"My Love"

RELEASE DATE 1968
ALBUM *Here's Loretta Lynn*

This was about the fifth song I wrote. I'd written one about my mommy and my daddy (besides "Coal Miner's Daughter"), so I thought since I was writing about the people I loved, how could I leave Doo out because he is "My Love." When I wrote the song it was early one morning, right after he had gone to work, and I was thinking how much I love him, and as far as I was concerned he might as well have been the only man in the world. I think this song speaks for itself because he forever will be "My Love."

**His sweet caress, his tenderness
His warm embrace, his gentle face
I love him so, I'll let him know
That he's my love.**

**Oh moon up there, show him I care
Give him my love, oh moon above
He'll always be the one for me
'Cause he's my love.**

Loretta and Mooney, late 1980s

"Whispering Sea"

RELEASE DATE 1968
ALBUM *Here's Loretta Lynn*

I sat down by the sea and it
  whispered to me
It brought back an old love affair
  that used to be
It told me that you had found
  someone new
And left me to cry over you

Whispering sea rolling by now
  don't you listen to me cry?
I cry as though my heart is broke in
  two
Oh how I love him so no one will
  ever know
No one but the drifting, whispering
  sea

Well I thought I'd left behind all his
  love, but I was blind
I should have known that there was
  no use to pretend
I thought a new love I would find
  and you would never cross my
  mind
But the whispering sea, it talked
  to me

Whispering sea rolling by now
  don't you listen to me cry
I cry as though my heart is broke in
  two
Oh how I love him so no one will
  ever know
No one but the drifting, whispering
  sea

No one but the drifting, whispering
  sea

"He's Somewhere Between You and Me"

WRITTEN WITH Doyle Wilburn
RELEASE DATE 1969
ALBUM *Your Squaw Is on the Warpath*

I don't know the location he's usin'
  he's so close and still I can't see
But I know all the heartache he's
  bringin' sure he's somewhere
  between you and me
When you say that you love me I
  don't doubt it
But he tells me the same things you
  see
All I know he's on my mind much
  too often 'cause he's somewhere
  between you and me
Yes he's somewhere between you
  and me give me time to erase his
  memory
'Cause my heart has to be free
  completely and he's somewhere
  between you and me

Yes he's somewhere . . .
Yes he's somewhere between you
  and me

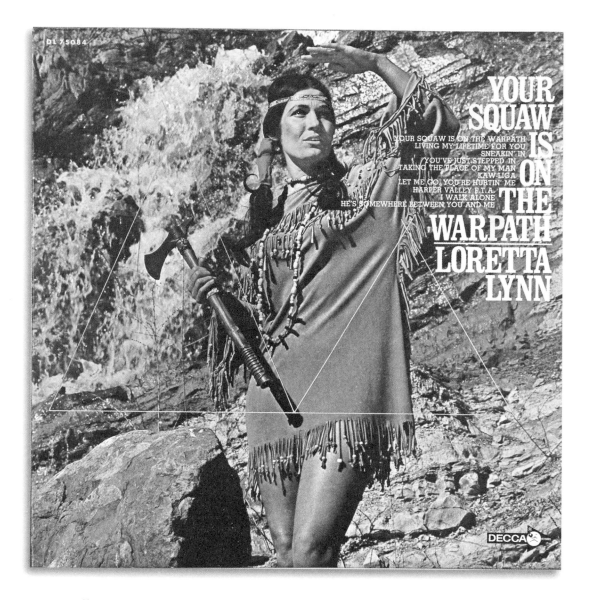

DL 75084

YOUR SQUAW IS ON THE WARPATH
LIVING MY LIFETIME FOR YOU
SNEAKIN' IN
YOU'VE JUST STEPPED IN
TAKING THE PLACE OF MY MAN
KAW-LIGA
LET ME GO, YOU'RE HURTIN' ME
HARPER VALLEY P.T.A.
I WALK ALONE
HE'S SOMEWHERE BETWEEN YOU AND ME

YOUR
SQUAW
IS
ON
THE
WARPATH
LORETTA
LYNN

DECCA

"Let Me Go You're Hurtin' Me"

WRITTEN WITH Lorene Allen
RELEASE DATE 1969
ALBUM *Your Squaw Is on the Warpath*

This is the first song Lorene and I ever wrote together. Lorene was my assistant for many years, as well as my best friend. I don't believe we are the only women who doubt, at times, whether our man loves us or not. A woman needs to know. So we just put our heads together, with both of us feeling the same way. Since we couldn't ask the men that we loved, we just wrote what we felt in this song. It might help others to know that we've been there, too. We've *all* been there. I always loved writing songs with Lorene because we knew each other so well. It was always easy and fun.

Let me go please let me go you're
hurtin' me
I've lost all your love so I can't
understand
Are you holdin' on to just show me
you can
This grip you have on me is as tight
as it can be
Let me go please let me go you're
hurtin' me
Stayin' here unwanted will be the
death of me
Needing love that you won't give
me so desperately
It's more than I can stand let me go
for I still can
Let me go please let me go you're
hurtin' me

Got no place to go but I'll go
anyway if I go I'll cry and I'll cry if
I stay
I still love you can't you see and I
don't want to be free
Let me go please let me go you're
hurtin' me
Stayin' here unwanted . . .

"Sneakin' In"

RELEASE DATE 1969
ALBUM *Your Squaw Is on the Warpath*

It's now three o'clock in the
morning the doorknob turns and
you tiptoe to bed
You think you're sneakin' in you
should know better
I know exactly what goes on inside
your head
You've been with the boys so you'll
tell me
It's a lie because I know right where
you've been
I followed you tonight and watched
you kiss her
Don't be so quiet 'cause you're not
sneakin' in
Next time you're sneakin' in ring
the doorbell
'Cause I won't be here to see the
shape you're in
I've been losin' lots of sleep over
nothin'
And I'm tired of hearin' nothin'
sneakin' in

And I'm tired of hearin' nothin'
sneakin' in

Fan club party, 1980s

"Your Squaw Is on the Warpath"

RELEASE DATE 1969
ALBUM *Your Squaw Is on the Warpath*

Most of you already know that on both sides of my family there were Indians. Many, many times when I was a little girl, if Mommy got a little mad about something, I would say to Daddy, "What's wrong with Mommy?" He would always say, "The squaw is on the warpath." When I would get mad at Doo about something, he would say the same thing. One time when I'd been on the road for about two weeks, I thought about what Daddy used to say and how Doo was doing it now. So I thought, "Hmmm, I'll write a song about it." I started on the song about ten p.m. one night and didn't finish it until three in the morning. Not thinking of the time, I called Doo up and said, "Oh honey, I've written a hit," all excited.

He said, "Yeah?"

I said, "I'm going to sing it to you." I started it out, and by the time I got to the chorus there was no one on the line but me. I still like the song and sometimes I *am* the "Squaw on the Warpath."

Well your pet name for me is
  Squaw
When you come home a drinkin'
  and can barely crawl
And all that lovin' on me won't
  make things right
Well you leave me at home to keep
  the teepee clean
Six papooses to break and then
  wean
Well your squaw is on the warpath
  tonight
Well I've found out a big brave
  chief the game you're a huntin'
  for ain't beef
Get off of my huntin' grounds and
  get out of my sight
This war dance I'm doin' means I'm
  fightin' mad
You don't need no more of what
  you've already had
Your squaw is on the warpath
  tonight

Well that fire-water that you've
  been drinking
Makes you feel bigger but chief
  you're shrinking
Since you've been on that
  lovemaking diet
Now don't hand me that ole peace
  pipe there ain't no pipe can settle
  this fight
Your squaw is on the warpath
  tonight
Well I've found out a big brave
  chief . . .
Yeah your squaw is on the warpath
  tonight

"Big Sister, Little Sister"

WRITTEN WITH Frances Irene Heighton
RELEASE DATE 1969
ALBUM *Woman of the World/To Make a
Man*

(Give up to the baby that's what
  they'd always say)
And big sister would let her have
  her way
We shared a sandbox little sister
  and me I was her big sister and
  she was only three
Give up to the baby that's what
  they'd always say
And big sister would let her have
  her way
All through our childhood and our
  high school days
My little sister always had to have
  her way
Now I can't hurt the baby and I
  can't let him go
Be brave big sister this time and
  say no
Now all that I remember as they
  drove out of sight
Just married and her holdin' the
  one I love so tight
Now all I do is rock my darling I just
  can't let her cry
So rock a bye baby rock a bye
Give up to the baby and I'd lose
  every time
Now they're saying big sister is
  losin' her mind

"I'm Lonesome for Trouble Tonight"

WRITTEN WITH Doyle Wilburn
RELEASE DATE 1969
ALBUM *Woman of the World/To Make a Man*

He's nothin' but trouble but he's
    always on my mind
I tried all I know to do to leave
    trouble behind
I can hardly live without him I even
    miss the fights
I'm lonesome for trouble tonight
I'm lonesome for trouble tonight
    and I ache for trouble's arms to
    hold me tight
Every time we get together seems
    like nothin' comes out right
Lord I'm lonesome for trouble
    tonight

Unhappy when I'm with him I'm
    unhappy when I'm not
I've tried so hard to get along but
    trouble's all I've got
It's hard to have somebody on your
    mind but out of sight
Yes I'm lonesome for trouble
    tonight
I'm lonesome for trouble . . .

"One Little Reason"

RELEASE DATE 1969
ALBUM *Woman of the World/To Make a Man*

There's a reason I keep living while
    I'm dyin' slow
Everybody thinks we're happy but
    we're not
I don't know why but I let him keep
    me cryin'
So I guess one little reason's all I've
    got.
When I lay me down to sleep I
    know I must wake up
And the reason that I do sure
    means a lot
Someday my reason will grow up
    and then will break up
For this one little reason's all I've
    got.
Little handprints on the wall, little
    footsteps in the hall
And little arms that reach out for
    me in the night
And when she says I love you so my
    mommy
I know this one little reason's my
    whole life.
Little handprints on the wall, little
    footsteps in the hall
And little arms that reach out for
    me in the night
And when she says I love you so my
    mommy
I know this one little reason's my
    whole life . . .

"The Only Time I Hurt"

RELEASE DATE 1969
ALBUM *Woman of the World/To Make a Man*

Now I know that I'll forget you
  'cause I forgot you a while ago
And when I thought of you just
  now only one tear dripped down
  slow
My mind is tired and twisted so and
  it hardly ever sleeps
But the only time I've hurt is when
  my heart beats

Since I'm finally gettin' over you I
  think I'll celebrate
Think of breakin' all your pictures
  and I might throw one away
And I won't feel this awful pain in
  about ten million weeks
'Cause the only time I hurt is when
  my heart beats

The only time I hurt is when my
  heart beats
I live in constant mis'ry 'cause the
  hurtin' just repeats
I think about you now and then and
  every time your mem'ry speaks
But the only time I hurt is when my
  heart beats

The only time I hurt is when my
  heart beats
I live in contant mis'ry 'cause the
  hurtin' just repeats
I think about you now and then and
  every time your mem'ry speaks
But the only time I hurt is when my
  heart beats.

"To Make a Man Feel Like a Man"

RELEASE DATE 1969
ALBUM *Woman of the World/To Make a Man*

The man I've got loves to be loved
  on and he likes to wear the
  britches
He don't like doin' women things
  like washin' clothes and dishes
You'll find he's not that hard to
  please if you love him right and
  fill his needs
To make a man feel like a man you
  gotta show him you're a woman

Show him what you are you know
  you can do it
Don't let some other woman come
  along and beat you to it
Lots of girls might catch his eye
  but what is a girl when a woman
  falls by
To make a man feel like a man you
  gotta show him you're a woman

When he comes home from a hard
  day's work he's probably tired
  and dirty
Don't let him find this latchy queen
  have your castle lookin' purty
There's lots of things that you
  shouldn't do like just as many
  that you should do too
To make a man feel like a man you
  gotta show him you're a woman

Show him what you are you know
  you can do it
Don't let some other woman come
  along and beat you to it

Lots of girls might catch his eye
   but what is a girl when a woman
   falls by
To make a man feel like a man you
   gotta show him you're a woman

To make a man feel like a man you
   gotta show him you're a woman

"If We Put Our Heads Together"

WRITTEN WITH Lorene Allen
RELEASE DATE 1969
ALBUM *Loretta Lynn and Ernest Tubb,
If We Put Our Heads Together*

When I'm cryin' just cryin' over
   what we've become
That's not but cry though I look
   there on the damage that we've
   done
We can start here not parted for
   there's hope for me and you
If we put our heads together our
   hearts will tell us what to do
If we put our heads together our
   hearts will tell us what to do
My heart tells me to forget her and
   I'll forget him too
I'll take a step in your direction and
   toward you I'll take two
If we put our heads together our
   hearts will tell us what to do

It's not rain it's just pain runnin'
   down my face
I feel certain that's a hurtin' won't
   leave any trace
We'll erase it just replace it with a
   love we once knew

If we put our heads together our
   hearts will tell us what to do
If we put our heads . . .

"I'm Gettin' Tired of Babyin' You"

WRITTEN WITH Peggy Sue Wells
RELEASE DATE 1969
ALBUM *Dynamite!* (released by
   Peggy Sue)

Well, you know how to treat me to
   get the things you want,
You whine just like a little bitty
   baby, if things don't go your way.
Well, I'm gonna break you, baby, if
   it's the last thing I do,
'Cause I'm a gettin' tired of babyin'
   you.

Yeah I'm a gettin' tired of babyin'
   you.
Once in a while would be OK but all
   the time won't do.
You go to bed with that ole bottle,
   and you get up with it too.
Yeah I'm a gettin' tired of babyin'
   you.

I'm gonna start with that ole
   bottle, I'm gonna drink it today
So, tonight when you start bawlin',
   you ain't a gonna get your way.
Well, I'm tired of baby-sittin' and I
   think it's time you knew.
That I'm a gettin' tired of babyin'
   you.

Yeah I'm a gettin' tired of babyin'
    you.
Once in a while would be OK but all
    the time won't do.
You go to bed with that ole bottle,
    and you make me number two.
Yeah I'm a gettin' tired of babyin'
    you.

"No Woman Can Hold Him Too Long"

WRITTEN WITH Peggy Sue Wells
RELEASE DATE 1969
ALBUM *Dynamite!* (released by
Peggy Sue)

He is as restless as a stormy night
No woman can hold him too long
He'll be all you can see, then he'll
    fall out of sight.
No woman can hold him too long
His love is so right, but he'll leave
    you so wrong
And he'll take what he wants in
    your arms.
Like a thief in the night, stealin'
    love, movin' on
No, no woman can hold him too
    long.

"You're Leavin' Me for Her Again"

WRITTEN WITH Peggy Sue Wells
RELEASE DATE 1969
ALBUM *Dynamite!* (released by
Peggy Sue)

You've got something on your mind
    you want to tell me,
And by the look on your face you
    think I'll hurt.
Don't be surprised if I don't cry, this
    ain't the end.
Yes I know, you're leavin' me for her
    again.

If she's got what it takes to make
    you happy,
I'm sorry she's got love that I'm
    without
No she don't love you, she's no
    good, she never has been
Yes I know you're leavin' me for her
    again.

Don't put it off, tell me now, let's
    get it over.
This ain't the first time, but it's the
    last time you're leavin' me for her
    again.
She'll drag you down and what a
    shame, for what you did
Oh yes I know you're leavin' me for
    her again.

The Seventies

Working on the road doing two hundred shows a year is hard. It takes its toll on you. It's hard on your family, too. By the late sixties and early seventies, it seemed like all I did was eat, sleep, sing, and ride. I stayed tired all the time, and my health was really paying the price for working so hard. When I did get to come home, it would be for only a day or so and Doolittle and the kids needed me to spend my time with them, so it was a very hard time for me to write. I think that's what happens to a lot of artists. They have great ideas and songs, but they get so busy they have no time to think, much less write. But I was able to write a few good songs here and there during these years, like "Rated X" and "You're Lookin' at Country."

"The Big Ole Hurt"

RELEASE DATE 1970
ALBUM *Wings upon Your Horns*

Well you've been a bouncin' me
    just like a rubber ball
And I'm a gettin' tired of bouncin'
    and that ain't all
I'm gonna see what I've been
    missin' I'm gonna start two-timin'
    too
Yeah I'm a gonna put the big ole
    hurt on you

I'm gettin' ready to put the big ole
    hurt on you
Gonna give you a little sample of
    what you've put me through
Now you can't stop me baby I'm
    gonna do what I want to do
Yeah I'm a gonna put the big ole
    hurt on you

What made you think you could
    love 'em all and still love me
I'm gonna show you just how
    hurtin' a hurt can be
'Cause I've been a one man's
    woman now I'm a gonna try for
    two
Yeah I'm a gonna put the big ole
    hurt on you

I'm gettin' ready to put the big ole
    hurt on you
Gonna give you a little sample of
    what you've put me through
Now you can't stop me baby I'm
    gonna do what I want to do
Yeah I'm a gonna put the big ole
    hurt on you

Right before a show, 1970s

"I Only See the Things I Wanna See"

WRITTEN WITH Loudilla Maxine Johnson
RELEASE DATE 1970
ALBUM *Wings upon Your Horns*

I can see you come to gossip and
    they tell me so and so
But there's not a thing about him I
    don't already know
I guess you think I'm crazy but it
    keeps him here with me
And I only see the things I wanna
    see
I only see the things I wanna see
    where he's concerned
It wouldn't do my heart no good
    believin' what I've learned
I can't face the truth about the man
    he'll never be
So I only see the things I wanna see

I only see the things I wanna see
    where he's concerned
It wouldn't do my heart much good
    believin' what I've learned
But it's worth all my heartaches
    when I have him here with me
So I only see the things I wanna see
    yes I only see the things I wanna
    see

Fall Fair, late 1980s

"I'm Dynamite"

RELEASE DATE 1970
ALBUM *Wings upon Your Horns*

I know you see that don't touch
    sign all over me
My pain is wet and you'll get hurt
    all over you
I'm another man's woman to you
    I'm just bad news
I'm dynamite so please don't light
    the fuse
You turn me on but I can't turn me
    off I guess the switch is buried in
    my mind

The flame of love is burning just
    begging to be used
I'm dynamite so please don't light
    the fuse
You can't undo the damage that I'll
    do and the first thing I'll destroy
    it will be you
Too many other hearts and vows
    that I can't stand to lose
I'm dynamite so please don't light
    the fuse

You can't undo the damage . . .
I'm dynamite so please don't light
    the fuse

"Let's Get Back Down to Earth"

RELEASE DATE 1970
ALBUM *Wings upon Your Horns*

Well this ol' world is a gettin' worse
   and worse every day
People livin' up above their heads
   and makin' bills that they can't
   pay
They're jealous of their neighbors
   and it's been like that since birth
So come on down and get your
   feet on the ground let's get back
   down to earth
Let's get back down to earth and
   live with the common people
Then we won't be miserable when
   we get old and feeble
Let's all be honest with ourselves
   we all know what we're worth
So come on down and get your
   feet on the ground let's get back
   down to earth

When we all come to this ol' world
   we didn't bring a thing
And when we all leave this ol'
   world we're gonna take the same
You'll be no better than I am when
   the man says dirt to dirt
So come on down and get your
   feet on the ground let's get back
   down to earth
Let's get back down to earth . . .
Come on down and get your feet on
   the ground let's get back down to
   earth

"When I Reach the Bottom"

WRITTEN WITH Lorene Allen
RELEASE DATE 1970
ALBUM *Wings upon Your Horns*

You want me to come down to your
   level you know that's pretty low
That looks like I will soon be there
   'cause I don't have very far to go
You turn my feet in your direction
   and I follow everywhere
So when I reach the bottom you'd
   better be there
I'm going down the ladder one step
   at a time
I'm going down the ladder that I'll
   never climb
You keep a saying come on down
   like a fool I ask you where
So when I reach the bottom you'd
   better be there

The road we're on is a going down
   the hill and I'm turning where you
   turn
You're teaching me your way of life
   and it didn't take me very long to
   learn
I'll do anything you want me to I've
   got to where I don't care
But when I reach the bottom you'd
   better be there
I'm going down the ladder . . .
So when I reach the bottom you'd
   better be there

"Wings upon Your Horns"

RELEASE DATE 1970
ALBUM *Wings upon Your Horns*

A lot of people say to me, "Loretta, you sure have accomplished a lot." Well, sometimes I ask myself: Why am I so driven to accomplish what I set out to do? The answer is because I know I must. When you love someone and they believe in you, you want to make them proud. This story may sound a little square to most of you today, but right after Doo and I got married I asked him, "Honey, why do the boys like best all the girls who do the wrong things?" So he took me by the hand and said, "Let me tell you something, Loretta. A man goes out with that kind for one thing. When it's time for him to get married, he tries very hard to find one like I did." I looked at him with much love, and in his eyes I saw someone who was very wise. So I wrote this song. All I did was go to my music room alone and close the door and try to be the girl in my mind with "Wings upon Your Horns."

Before you first made love to me
you called me your wife to be
And after that I saw the devil in
your eyes
With your sweet smooth-talkin'
ways you turned a flame into a
blaze
Then I'd've let you hang my wings
upon your horns
Don't tell me that I'm no saint I'm
the first to know I ain't
There's a little thing called love and
that's what changed me
From an innocent country girl to a
woman of the world
Then I'd've let you hang my wings
upon your horns
You hung my wings upon your
horns and turned my halo into
thorns
And turned me to a woman I can't
stand
You're the first who ever made me
fall in love and then not take me
Then I'd've let you hang my wings
upon your horns
You hung my wings upon your
horns . . .

OPPOSITE Backstage at the
Opry, 1970s

"You Wouldn't Know an Angel"

WRITTEN WITH Frances Rhodes
RELEASE DATE 1970
ALBUM *Wings upon Your Horns*

Because I won't give in to you, you
    don't treat me like you should
You said that I'm too perfect then
    you tell me I'm no good
But everyone is guilty of sometimes
    doin' wrong
But even so you wouldn't know an
    angel if you saw one

No you wouldn't know an angel if
    you saw one
You won't see any halos on the
    women found in bars
I may not get to heaven but I'm not
    the only one
To tell you so you wouldn't know an
    angel if you saw one

Now you stand there accusing me
    of things you always do
And half the things you're telling
    me are things I never knew
I don't go places you go but that's
    your way of fun
It goes to show you wouldn't know
    an angel if you saw one

No you wouldn't know an angel if
    you saw one
You won't see any halos on the
    women found in bars
I may not get to heaven but I'm not
    the only one
To tell you so you wouldn't know an
    angel if you saw one

"Crazy Out of My Mind"

RELEASE DATE 1970
ALBUM *Loretta Lynn Writes 'Em and Sings 'Em*

I'm to the place where I don't know
    my name
It's a world for the lonely go insane
I've brought along the little pieces
    of me he left behind
Got no place to go but crazy out of
    my mind

I've got no place to go but crazy out
    of my mind over baby
He's the last thing I remember that
    I won't forget in time
Got no place to go but crazy out of
    my mind

I've watched him leave with hurt
    clear out of sight
And from that day on my mind just
    don't work right
What little sense left in me I'll leave
    here in this wine
Got no place to go but crazy out of
    my mind

I've got no place to go but crazy out
    of my mind over baby
He's the last thing I remember that
    I won't forget in time
Got no place to go but crazy out of
    my mind

"Deep as Your Pocket"

RELEASE DATE 1970
ALBUM *Loretta Lynn Writes 'Em and Sings 'Em*

You're tellin' me she loves you what
  a laugh
The funny thing is baby you don't
  know the half
If you've got any money honey
  you better put it in the safe and
  lock it
'Cause her love for you's just deep
  as your pocket
She's a too big girl in a fifty-dollar
  dress
She wouldn't think about wearin'
  anything that costs much less
I can see she rows a boat but little
  ol' me's gonna rock it
'Cause her love for you's just deep
  as your pocket
Yeah her love for you's just deep as
  your pocket
She's got you blown up like a
  balloon and I'm a gonna pop it
She can't love you like I do but
  don't let me to drop it
'Cause her love for you's just deep
  as your pocket

Yeah her love for you's . . .
Yeah her love for you's just deep as
  your pocket

"What's the Bottle Done to My Baby"

RELEASE DATE 1970
ALBUM *Loretta Lynn Writes 'Em and Sings 'Em*

We used to talk and plan of what
  we'd do but now you let the
  bottle talk for you
But I still love the man you used to
  be oh what's the bottle done to
  my baby
What's the bottle done to my baby
I've watched your mind go with
  that beer and whiskey flow
It's awful oh it's awful what a
  shame what's the bottle done to
  my baby

Back before the bottle took
  command I tell the world I loved
  its biggest man
But you've knocked all the pride
  right out of me
Oh what's the bottle done to my
  baby

What's the bottle done to my baby
I've watched your mind go with
  that beer and whiskey flow
It's awful oh it's awful what a
  shame what's the bottle done to
  my baby

Loretta and June Carter,
1985

"I Know How"

RELEASE DATE 1970
ALBUM *Loretta Lynn Writes 'Em and Sings 'Em*

This was Johnny Cash's favorite song. When he asked me to do his TV show, he asked me to sing "I Know How."

This was a fun song to write. I do have some blues in me, and, boy, I was really blues'ing this song up when I brought it in and sang it to Owen Bradley. Owen started laughing at me and said, "Loretta, honey, I love the song but maybe we should try and cut it a little more country." Well, he was probably right, but, nevertheless, I still sang it as bluesy as I could. Well, as blues as Owen would let me. Ha!

Yeah I love him like he wants me to
and I know how
And it's my duty to know his moods
when he gets moody
Yeah I give him what he needs and
that's why I'm his right now
Yes I know I love him right 'cause I
know how yeah I know how
Yes I know how to hold him when
he needs holdin'
And I know how to kiss him when
he needs kissin'
I understand his every wish and his
every wish is mine
Yes he knows I love to love him and
I know how yeah I know how

Yes I know how to hold him . . .
You better believe I know how

"One You Need"

RELEASE DATE 1970
ALBUM *Loretta Lynn Writes 'Em and Sings 'Em*

I'm not sayin' you don't love me
    'cause I know you do
But I have said enough to know you
    play some too
You tear me all to pieces then you
    asked me not to bleed
I'm the woman that you want but
    I'm not the one you need
The woman that you need is good
    for any ol' good time
And the woman that you want you
    wouldn't want if she's that kind
It hurts when you go sowin' wasted
    love from your wild seed
I'm the woman that you want but
    I'm not the one you need

The woman that you need . . .

"You Wanna Give Me a Lift"

RELEASE DATE 1970
ALBUM *Loretta Lynn Writes 'Em and Sings 'Em*

Well I'm game for just about
    anything but the game you've
    named I ain't gonna play
You say you take a little drink and
    we'll go for a ride on a star
You wanna give me a lift but this ol'
    gal ain't a goin' that far
That happy pill you're takin' you say
    is a little weak
And you wanna give me one so you
    say I won't go to sleep
Well your hands're a gettin' friendly
    but I know exactly where they
    are
You wanna give me a lift but this ol'
    gal ain't a goin' that far
You wanna give me a lift but this ol'
    gal ain't a goin' that far

Loretta at the South
Dakota American Indian
School, 1970s

79

I'm a little bit warm but that don't mean I'm on fire
You wanna take me for a ride in the backseat of your car
You wanna give me a lift but this ol' gal ain't a goin' that far

You wanna give me a lift . . .
You wanna give me a lift but this ol' gal ain't a goin' that far

"Another Man Loved Me Last Night"

WRITTEN WITH Lorene Allen
RELEASE DATE 1970
ALBUM *Coal Miner's Daughter*

He doesn't know that I can't look him in the eyes
For that I can't speak or I'll just start tellin' lies
I hope he thinks that I'm just moody and quiet
But another man loved me last night

Yes, another man loved me last
  night
I'd almost forgotten what love was
  really like
But I'm only human only a woman
I let another man love me last night

While he's sleeping, well, I'm crying
  here awake
Not being loved was more than I
  could take
Thought it was wrong there in his
  arms it seemed so right
When another man loved me last
  night

Yes, another man loved me last
  night
I'd almost forgotten what love was
  really like
But I'm only human only a woman
I let another man love me last night

I released my heart my soul . . .
Do I wanna be free
Did I wanna be free?
Yeah, I wanna be free

"Any One, Any Worse, Any Where"

WRITTEN WITH Lorene Allen
RELEASE DATE 1970
ALBUM *Coal Miner's Daughter*

You're tellin' me how bad I am for
  loving him
That I can't be much and love him
  he's your man
Go on say I'm no good call me
  anything you dare

For if how much I love him tells
  how bad I am
Then you won't find anyone, any
  worse, anywhere

I treat him like the man he is and
  when he needs me I'm there
He must not think that I'm so bad
  for he takes me everywhere
For if how much I love him tells
  how bad I am
Then you won't find anyone, any
  worse, anywhere

You're tellin' me that you will never
  set him free
And you say that we've disgraced
  you him and me
You know you don't love him and
  he knows how much I care
So if how much I love him tells how
  bad I am
Then you won't find anyone, any
  worse, anywhere

I treat him like the man he is and
  when he needs me I'm there
He must not think that I'm so bad
  for he takes me everywhere
But if how much I love him tells
  how bad I am
Then you won't find anyone, any
  worse, anywhere

I was borned a cole miners Doughter
in a cobom on a Hill in Butcher
Holler.
I'm Proud to be a cole minis
Doughter.
and we washed our wash. from
a Pool of cold spring water.

My dodie worked all night in
the Van Lear cole mine.
most of the day in the field Hoeing
corn. Momma rocked the
babys at night read us
the bible from the lamp light
and we then
would start all over at the
freak of morn,

dodie loved and raised 8 kids
on mines Poy.
and momma scrubed our cloths on
wash forbed our day.
I seen her fingers bleed. to
complain well thire was no need.
and from the garden she d can
our food for a rainy day.

"Coal Miner's Daughter"

RELEASE DATE 1970
ALBUM *Coal Miner's Daughter*

I was out at Channel 2 doing *The Wilburn Brothers Show* when I wrote this song. I started this as a bluegrass song for the Osborne Brothers, but by the time I finished the first line I said, "Hey, that's not going to do. They can't be coal miner's daughters—what's wrong with me?" Before the song ended I had fourteen verses. I wrote about a lot of things that happened to me as I was growing up. My friend and producer, Owen Bradley, said, "Loretta, what's wrong with you? There has already been an 'El Paso.' There ain't gonna be another one. This song is long enough to be an album all by itself."

So, I had to get to work and take out eight verses, which was one of the hardest things I had to do with one of my songs because each verse meant something very personal about my life.

Well I was born a coal miner's
 daughter
In a cabin on a hill in Butcher Holler
We were poor, but we had love
That's the one thing Daddy made
 sure of

He shoveled coal to make a poor
 man's dollar

My Daddy worked all night in the
 Van Lear Coal Mines,
All day long in a field a-hoein' corn,
Mommy rocked the babies at night,
And read the Bible by the coal-oil
 light,
And everything would start all over
 come break of mornin'

Daddy loved and raised eight kids
 on a miner's pay
Mommy scrubbed our clothes on a
 washboard every day
Why, I've seen her fingers bleed, to
 complain, there was no need,
She'd smile in Mommy's
 understanding way

In the summertime we didn't have
 shoes to wear

But in the wintertime, we'd all get
a brand-new pair,
From a mail-order catalog, money,
made from sellin' a hog
Daddy always managed to get the
money somewhere

Yeah, I'm proud to be a coal miner's
daughter,
I remember well the well where I
drew water,
The work we done was hard at
night we'd sleep 'cause we were
tired,
I never thought of ever leavin'
Butcher Holler

Well, a lot of things have changed
since way back then
And it's so good to be back home
again,
Not much left but the floor, nothin'
lives here anymore
'Cept the memories of a coal
miner's daughter

"What Makes Me Tick"

RELEASE DATE 1970
ALBUM *Coal Miner's Daughter*

Gonna have my head examin'
'cause my mind's in bad shape
The way that you've been actin' I
think that you've gone ape
The way I let you treat me it's
enough to make me sick
I'm gonna have my head examin'
and find out what makes me tick
If I had the brains of a dummy I'd be
smart
'Cause there ain't no feelin' in a
poor dummy's heart
And when it comes to cheatin' well
honey you know every trick
I'm gonna have my head examin'
and find out what makes me tick

Gonna have my head examin'
'cause I know my mind is broke
Tonight I saw you kiss her you said
can't you take a joke
Now I won't be your monkey you'd
better change and quick
I'm gonna have my head examin'
and find out what makes me tick
If I had the brains . . .
I'm gonna have my head examin'
and find out what makes me tick

"Don't Tell Me You're Sorry"

RELEASE DATE 1970
ALBUM *Loretta Lynn and Conway Twitty, We Only Make Believe*

I'm sorry honey that you walked in
    and caught her in my lap
But it's not what you're thinking so
    think before you slap
I suppose you're weighin' that little
    blonde that walked here in this
    bar
Ah don't tell me you're sorry 'cause
    I know how sorry you are
I'm sorry that you think I'm drunk I
    ain't had a drink today
Would you believe I held her just to
    see how much she'd weigh
That cheatin' look that's on your
    face is lit up like a star

So don't tell me you're sorry 'cause I
    know how sorry you are
Don't tell me you're sorry but I'm as
    sorry as I can be
Well you'd better move fast and
    don't give me no sass 'cause you
    belong to me
Now honey we ain't done nothing
    wrong but I'm sorry it's gone this
    far
But don't tell me you're sorry 'cause
    I know how sorry you are

Don't tell me you're sorry . . .
Now wait a minute Loretta you
    know how sorry I am
Conway you better believe I know
    how sorry you are

"Romeo"

WRITTEN WITH Peggy Sue Wells
RELEASE DATE 1970
ALBUM *All American Husband*
(released by Peggy Sue)

The girls all say you're a Romeo,
  well I found out this is so
This ain't Rome and I ain't gonna do
  what the Romans do
I'll admit you got what it takes to
  make my poor heart shiver and
  shake
And I'd love to be your woman,
  Romeo.

You got Roman hands and Russian
   fingers,
But honey bees die when they lose
   their stingers.
You know the kind of chicks you
   can buzz around with.
It's not that I don't love you, honey,
   to lose my pride wouldn't be too
   funny
But this Juliet really loves you,
   Romeo.

Your kisses set my heart on fire,
   gives my mind just one big jar
Mama told me to watch for times
   like this.
You're tellin' me that I'm a square,
   old-fashioned girls don't get
   nowhere,
You know I'm not that stupid,
   Romeo.

You got Roman hands and Russian
   fingers,
But honey bees die when they lose
   their stingers.
You know the kind of chicks you
   can buzz around with.
It's not that I don't love you, honey,
   to lose my pride wouldn't be too
   funny
But this Juliet really loves you,
   Romeo.

"Drive You Outta My Mind"

WRITTEN WITH Lorene Allen
RELEASE DATE 1971
ALBUM *I Wanna Be Free*

I know I shouldn't bother you 'cause
   you asked me not to call
But tonight I'm not responsible for
   what I do at all
You're drivin' me outta my mind is
   that what you want to do
Well do me a little favor and drive
   you out of my mind too
Drive you outta my mind erase the
   mem'ry of your touch
I don't believe I'm askin' for too
   much
You're drivin' me outta my mind
   and you know this is true
Well do me a little favor and drive
   you outta my mind too

Now don't tell me you don't have
   time 'cause the problems just
   can't wait
If I'll wait until tomorrow it just
   might be too late
You're drivin' me out of my mind by
   lovin' someone new
So do me a little favor and drive
   you outta my mind too
Drive you outta my mind . . .

"I Wanna Be Free"

RELEASE DATE 1971
ALBUM *I Wanna Be Free*

For twenty-five years my two tour buses have been my home away from home. And the day I wrote "I Wanna Be Free," we had been on the road about six weeks. Very seldom do I open the curtain in the back of my bus and look out, and why I did this day I don't know. But when I left to go on tour, the leaves had just started turning red and yellow. I was kind of down because I had been away from my babies and Doo for so long. When I looked out, the leaves had fallen to the ground, and the trees were bare. It made me realize just how long I'd been gone. I picked up the old guitar and started strumming. My first line was, "Well, I look out the window and what do I see?" Now, it's up to you to read the rest of the song.

Well I look out the window and
    what do I see?
The breeze is a blowin' the leaves
    from the trees everything is free
    everything but me
I'm gonna take this chain from
    around my finger
And throw it just as far as I can sling
    'er 'cause I wanna be free
When my baby left me everything
    died
But a little bluebird was singin' just
    outside singin' twiddle-de-dee fly
    away with me
Well you know I think I'm a gonna
    live gotta lotta love left in me to
    give
So I wanna be free
I released my heart my soul and my
    mind and I'm a feelin' fine
I broke the chains the ring of gold
    before it broke my mind
Well look who's cryin' and it ain't
    me but I can't hardly hear and I
    can't half see
Oh I wanna be free
I released my heart my soul . . .
Do I wanna be free yeah I wanna be
    free free

"I'm One Man's Woman"

WRITTEN WITH Peggy Sue Wells
RELEASE DATE 1971
ALBUM *I Wanna Be Free*

You know that I love you my love
   made me your fool
For way down deep inside I know
   you never will be true
But I'll keep holdin' on for love just
   as long as I can
I'm one man's woman but you're
   any woman's man
I'm one man's woman but you're
   any woman's man
But I can't let that change me into
   somethin' I can't stand
I give you all the love I have but
   your love is out of hand
I'm one man's woman but you're
   any woman's man

Sometimes I have a notion to get
   revenge but then
Since I'm in love who cares about
   the place I've never been
When temptation smiled at me
   into your arms I ran
I'm one man's woman but you're
   any woman's man
I'm one man's woman . . .

"If I Never Love Again (It'll Be Too Soon)"

WRITTEN WITH Teddy Wilburn
RELEASE DATE 1971
ALBUM *I Wanna Be Free*

All the heartaches that I've known
   would fill the sea
Call out lonesome and you'll be
   callin' me yeah callin' me
Oh mem'ries fill my little lonely
   room
And if I never love again it'll be too
   soon
Been left hurtin' by each love I've
   ever had
And your leavin' hurt the worst it
   hurt so bad it hurt me bad
Ohh misery cast its shadow on the
   moon
And if I never love again it'll be too
   soon
I don't wanna see another road
   than blue
And if I never love again it'll be too
   soon
I don't wanna ever see another
   road than blue
And if I never never love again it'll
   be too soon

"You're Lookin' at Country"

RELEASE DATE 1971
ALBUM *You're Lookin' at Country*

When I come home from off tour, Doo always shows me around and introduces me to all the new colts, new ducks, baby goats, and all. One time, I'd come back, and I got in the jeep and was riding around the ranch at Hurricane Mills, Tennessee, where I live. I looked over our hundred-acre field where Doo had some of his horses running around. It was in the spring, and everything was turning green. It was so beautiful, and I said to Doo, "You're lookin' at country, real country." I knew it was a good song title, but I also knew if I didn't write about a country boy and girl in love, it wouldn't be very commercial. I worked with the song off and on for about a week. You must have liked it 'cause you made it a hit.

Well I like my lovin' done country
    style and this little girl would
    walk a country mile
To find her a good ole slow-talkin'
    country boy I said a country boy
I'm about as old-fashioned as I can
    be and I hope you're likin' what
    you see
'Cause if you're lookin' at me you're
    lookin' at country

You don't see no city when you look
    at me 'cause country's all I am
I love runnin' barefooted through
    the old cornfields and I love that
    country ham
Well you say I'm made just to fit
    your plans
But does a barnyard shovel fit your
    hands?
If your eyes are on me you're
    lookin' at country

This here country is a little green
    and there's a lotta country that
    you ain't seen
I'll show you around if you'll show
    me a weddin' band I said a
    weddin' band
When it comes to love well I know
    about that country folks all know
    where it's at
If you're lookin' at me you're lookin'
    at country

You don't see no city when you look
    at me 'cause country's all I am
I love runnin' barefooted through
    the old cornfields and I love that
    country ham

OPPOSITE Long Horn
Rodeo, 1970s

Mooney, 1976

91

Well you say I'm made just to fit
    your plans
But does a barnyard shovel fit your
    hands?
If your eyes are on me you're
    lookin' at country

"Close My Eyes"

RELEASE DATE 1971
ALBUM *You're Lookin' at Country*

I know he knows I'm dead so why
    don't he close my eyes
'Cause as long as they stay open I
    can see where my heart lies
It's buried at his feet and when he
    steps on it it cries
Everybody knows I'm dead so why
    don't they close my eyes

My blue eyes are open wide and I
    can see her take my place
I know still I can feel the dirt he's
    throwin' in my face
He was every breath I breathe so
    how could I survive
Everybody knows I'm dead so why
    don't they close my eyes

My blue eyes are open wide and I
    can see her take my place
I know still I can feel the dirt he's
    throwin' in my face
He was every breath I breathe so
    how could I survive
Everybody knows I'm dead so why
    don't they close my eyes

"From Now On"

RELEASE DATE 1970
ALBUM *You're Lookin' at Country*

Lately when you kiss me, your lips
    are just lukewarm
There's a bored look on your face
    when you hold me in your arms
You act like it's your duty to love
    me when you do
But from now on, when you're
    lovin' me, you better act like
    you're wantin' to

You been gettin' your lovin'
    someplace else and I know it
But I'm gonna give you one more
    chance, so you better not blow it
You better shape up or start
    shippin' out, big man, I'm warnin'
    you
But from now on, when you're
    lovin' on me, you better act like
    you're wantin' to

I've noticed now for quite a while
    when I talk you don't hear
You stare out into space and you
    act like you don't hear,
But I ache for arms to hold me, I'm
    human just like you
But from now on, when you're
    lovin' on me, you better act like
    you're wantin' to.

You been a gettin' your lovin'
    someplace else and I know it
But I'm gonna give you one more
    chance, so you better not blow it
You better shape up or start
    shippin' out, big man, I'm warnin'
    you

Love whatcha got at home and quit
   that messin' around
Well everybody calls you lover boy
   and you like the way it sounds
Your home chores are never done
   because you're always gone
Well tonight big boy you're gonna
   stay right here and love whatcha
   got at home

But from now on, when you're
   lovin' on me, you better act like
   you're wantin' to
Yea from now on, when you're
   lovin' on me, you better act like
   you're wantin' to.

"Love Whatcha Got at Home"

WRITTEN WITH Peggy Sue Wells
RELEASE DATE 1971
ALBUM *You're Lookin' at Country*

Well you say you're a red hot papa
   and the lover over town
Don't you think it's just about time
   ole momma cools you down
Get them courtin' clothes back off
   don't let it take you long
'Cause tonight big boy you're
   gonna stay right here and love
   whatcha got at home

Well I watch TV till it goes off and
   then I count sheep
I never know when you come home
   I cry myself to sleep
When you go out that door tonight
   consider yourself grown
'Cause tonight big boy you're
   gonna stay right here and love
   whatcha got at home

Love whatcha got at home and quit
   that messin' around
Well everybody calls you lover boy
   and you like the way it sounds
Your home chores are never done
   because you're always gone

Loretta and Mooney, 1988

Well tonight big boy you're gonna stay right here and love whatcha got at home

Well tonight big boy you're gonna stay right here and love whatcha got at home

Loretta in her tour bus,
1980

"I Feel Like Traveling On"

RELEASE DATE 1972
ALBUM *God Bless America Again*

My heavenly home is bright and
    fair
I feel like traveling on
No pain nor death can enter there
I feel like traveling on

Yes, I feel like traveling on I feel like
    traveling on
My heavenly home is bright and
    fair I feel like traveling on

It's glittering towers of sun
   outshines
I feel like traveling on
That heavenly mansion shall be
   mine
I feel like traveling on

Yes, I feel like traveling on I feel like
   traveling on
My heavenly home is bright and
   fair I feel like traveling on.

The Lord has been so good to me
I feel like traveling on
Until that blessed home I see
I feel like traveling on

Yes, I feel like traveling on I feel like
   traveling on
My heavenly home is bright and
   fair I feel like traveling on.

"I Miss You More Today"

WRITTEN WITH Lorene Allen
RELEASE DATE 1972
ALBUM *Here I Am Again*

Today I tried to think things
   through, tryin' to get over you
But I've been thinkin' ever since
   you went away
Every thought is one that hurts and
   each day that hurt gets worse
And I miss you more today than
   yesterday

I miss you more today than
   yesterday

I had always heard it works the
   other way
Someone said that time heals
   sorrow
But I can't help but dread tomorrow
When I miss you more today than
   yesterday

Today I thought I'd try to smile,
   since you've been gone for quite
   a while
But memory says there'll be no
   smiles today
I doubt that I could ever find peace
   of mind in spite of time
'Cause I miss you more today than
   yesterday

I miss you more today than
   yesterday
I had always heard it works the
   other way
Someone said that time heals
   sorrow
But I can't help but dread tomorrow
When I miss you more today than
   yesterday

"LOVE"

WRITTEN WITH Maggie Vaughn
RELEASE DATE 1972
ALBUM *One's on the Way*

L-o-v-e l-o-v-e love
There couldn't be a bad word I
   haven't heard you say
Don't you know the needs of any
   woman
You speak words my ears have
   never heard of

The only four-letter word that you
   don't know is l-o-v-e love

L-o-v-e a word you never use l-o-v-e
   your lips never choose
It's enough to make a woman want
   to give up
The only four-letter word that you
   don't know is l-o-v-e love

It would tear me all to pieces if you
   ever came to me
With more to give than one robbed
   kiss at nighttime
You'll never know the longing that
   my heart does
The only four-letter word that you
   don't know is l-o-v-e love

L-o-v-e a word you never use l-o-v-e
   your lips never choose
It's enough to make a woman want
   to give up
The only four-letter word that you
   don't know is l-o-v-e love

"Five Fingers Left"

RELEASE DATE 1973
ALBUM *Love Is the Foundation*

Once upon a time I had a real good
   friend, at least that's what I
   thought,
But it wasn't long till my good
   friend and the man I love got
   caught.
So, who in the world is a foolin'
   who? Let's not kid ourselves.

We can count our friends on one
   hand, and have five fingers left.

Friends are few and far between,
   believe me, I should know.
And a real good way to find it out is
   to let no money show.
So, who in the world is a foolin'
   who? Let's not kid ourselves.
We can count our friends on one
   hand, and have five fingers left.

When you're down and out and you
   need a friend, you'll find they're
   hard to find.
And when you do, don't turn your
   back, 'cause your friend will rob
   you blind.
So, who in the world is foolin' who?
   Let's not kid ourselves.
We can count our friends on one
   hand, and have five fingers left.

We all know what our enemies will
   do, it's our friends we have to
   watch.
Keep your eyes open and your big
   mouth shut, and you'll find out a
   lot.
So, who in the world is foolin' who?
   Let's not kid ourselves.
We can count our friends on one
   hand, and have five fingers left.

"I Pray My Way Outta Trouble"

WRITTEN WITH Teddy Wilburn
RELEASE DATE 1972
ALBUM God Bless America Again

Many times my mind is wrapped up
    in trouble and my heart gets so
    heavy too
Sometimes when I sink so low I
    touch bottom
I kneel down to reach out and He
    pulls me through
I pray my way out of trouble and I
    ask my dear Lord to help me each
    day
I pray my way out of trouble and
    the dear nail-scarred hand wipes
    my teardrops away

The smallest prayer from the
    world's biggest sinner brings a
    smile to His saddened face
So I just go to Him any time I am in
    trouble
Wash my heart in the waters of my
    Saviour's grace
I pray my way . . .

"Working for the Lord"

RELEASE DATE 1972
ALBUM God Bless America Again

The Bible is our weapon, the
    ammunition inside
I'm told, let's go fight on Jesus' side,
    He hasn't lost one soul.
Let's join His band of soldiers 'cause
    they don't live by the sword,

We'll be fighting for our
    countrymen, but we'll be working
    for the Lord.

Sixteen years ago today, I gave
    birth to a little boy
And all the worries I had for him,
    every minute has been a joy.
And when they laid him in my arms,
    on that twenty-seventh day of
    May
I looked down at his tiny little face,
    and you should have heard me
    pray
"Oh dear God you've blessed me
    with more than I deserve,
And someday, God, when he grows
    up, it's you I'll pray he'll serve."

Now, all his friends have gathered
    around to help him celebrate,
He just blew out the candles and
    has begun to cut the cake.
They're laughin' and they're talking
    of what they're gonna do and be
    someday
And when they get a little older,
    they're going to fight for their
    country,
But I couldn't help but overhear
    what my son had to say;
And there's not one doubt in my
    mind that my prayer paid off
    today.

"Rated X"

RELEASE DATE 1973
ALBUM *Entertainer of the Year*

This song, I think, was kind of taken wrong by some women. Some wrote me and said I was looking down on divorced women. If they had listened real good, they would have got the story right. I was taking up for divorced women. Once you have been married, if you got divorced or became widowed, every man takes it for granted that you're available, that you're easy. Maybe it's because they think that because we've been through so much, we're just ready for fun. They don't understand that while some women are like that, most aren't. That was the story I was trying to tell—I was talking to the men, trying to set them straight. I thought the title was great, and I tried hard to put the right story to the song. I remember when I first wrote and recorded "Rated X," I did the TV show *Hee Haw*. After the show was on the air, we got some mail saying the song was dirty and putting down women. But that is one thing I'll never do.

Well if you've been a married
  woman and things didn't seem to
  work out
Divorce is the key to bein' loose and
  free so you're gonna be talked
  about

Everybody knows that you've loved
  once so they think you'll love again
You can't have a male friend when
  you're a has-been or a woman
  you're rated X

And if you're rated X you're some
  kind of goal every man might try
  to make
But I think it's wrong to judge every
  picture if a cheap camera makes a
  mistake
And when your best friend's
  husband says to you you've sure
  started lookin' good
You should've known he would and
  he would if he could and he will if
  you're rated X

Well nobody knows where you're
  goin' but they sure know where
  you've been
All they're thinkin' of is your
  experience of love their minds eat
  up with sin
The women all look at you like
  you're bad and the men all hope
  you are
But if you go too far you're gonna
  wear the scar of a woman rated X

And if you're rated X you're some
  kind of goal every man might try
  to make
But I think it's wrong to judge every
  picture if a cheap camera makes a
  mistake
And when your best friend's
  husband says to you you've sure
  started lookin' good
You should've known he would and
  he would if he could and he will if
  you're rated X

OPPOSITE Loretta on *Hee Haw,* 1980

Coal Miners Music

By the early seventies so many things had changed in my life. I had been recording for a while, had a few pretty big records, and was doing pretty good. Doo and I had left the Wilburns and started our own company called Loretta Lynn Enterprises. Leaving the Wilburns was very hard for me to do. We were all so close. But it was time. And it was the right thing for me and Doo. I wanted to start my own publishing company as well. I always loved being around songwriters, watching how they thought and worked. So with the help of a few friends, I started Coal Miners Music Group. At one time I had about twelve songwriters writing for me. I recorded a lot of songs in my publishing company and had a lot of other artists recording them as well. We had quite a few number one hits. Of all my businesses, I am most proud of my publishing company.

"Since I've Got the Pill"

WRITTEN WITH Lorene Allen, T. D. Bayless, Don McHan
RELEASE DATE 1975
ALBUM *Back to the Country*

You wined me and dined me
When I was your girl
Promised if I'd be your wife
You'd show me the world
But all I've seen of this old world
Is a bed and a doctor bill
I'm tearin' down your brooder
    house
'Cause now I've got the pill.
All these years I've stayed at home
While you had all your fun
And every year that's gone by
Another baby's come
There's gonna be some changes
    made
Right here on nursery hill
You've set this chicken your last
    time
'Cause now I've got the pill.
This old maternity dress I've got
Is goin' in the garbage
The clothes I'm wearin' from now
    on
Won't take up so much yardage
Miniskirts, hot pants and a few
    little fancy frills
Yeah I'm makin' up for all those
    years
Since I've got the pill.
I'm tired of all your crowin'
How you and your hens play
While holdin' a couple in my arms
Another's on the way.
This chicken's done tore up her nest
And I'm ready to make a deal

And you can't afford to turn it
    down
'Cause you know I've got the pill.
This incubator is overused
Because you've kept it filled
The feelin' good comes easy now
Since I've got the pill.
It's getting dark it's roostin' time
Tonight's too good to be real
Oh but Daddy don't you worry
    none
'Cause Mama's got the pill
Oh Daddy don't you worry none
'Cause Mama's got the pill.

"Red, White, and Blue"

RELEASE DATE 1976
ALBUM *When the Tingle Becomes a Chill*

This song was written about Mommy. Her daddy was Cherokee Indian. Her mamma was a little redheaded Irish girl who came over on the boat from Ireland when she was only three years old. I never did get to see my grandmother, because she died very young while having twins, from what they called "childbed fever" back then. My mother and her twin sister were only five years old when their mamma died. As for the blue, I guess all young girls in love are blue at times. The only thing in this song that is not true is where I say, "I did before I said I do," because I didn't. My husband and I had a home in Mexico, and that's where I started writing this song. We used to take our own twins and spend the winters down there. My twins still laugh and tell the story of how no one could speak English in the little village we lived in. But by the time we left that winter, everyone in town was all singing, "I'm red, white, and blue ah-ooh ah-ooh."

I'm red white and blue ah-ooh,
    ah-ooh, ah-ooh
Ah-ooh, ah-ooh, ah-ooh and I'm
    proud of it too
The red come from my grandpa he's
    an all-American brave
The white come from my grandma
    she's a redhead Irish maid
The blue come from the man I love
    'cause I did before I said I do
    ah-ooh
That leaves me a mixed-up breed of
    red, white and blue

I'm red white and blue ah-ooh,
    ah-ooh, ah-ooh
Ah-ooh, ah-ooh, ah-ooh and I'm
    proud of it too
I'm a blue-eyed Indian squaw
    everybody calls me a half breed

That's what you get when you sow
    a little red and a white seed
The white man said he'd marry me
    he lied 'cause babies do ah-ooh
That leaves me a mixed-up breed of
    red, white and blue

I'm red white and blue ah-ooh,
    ah-ooh, ah-ooh
Ah-ooh, ah-ooh, ah-ooh and I'm
    proud of it too
The great white fathers had it
    planned to take the red man's
    land
I think you think I'm prejudiced but
    I'd never lie to you
There's war-red blood running
    through my veins and I wish my
    skin was too
I wish my skin was too
I'm red white and blue ah-ooh,
    ah-ooh, ah-ooh
Ah-ooh, ah-ooh, ah-ooh
I'm red white and blue ah-ooh,
    ah-ooh, ah-ooh
Ah-ooh, ah-ooh, ah-ooh
I'm red white and blue ah-ooh,
    ah-ooh, ah-ooh
Ah-ooh, ah-ooh, ah-ooh

Crystal Gayle

My baby sister Brenda—all of you know her as Crystal Gayle. She was the last of eight kids, and yes, she is the baby of the family and she won't let you forget it. Ha! By the time Brenda (Crystal) was born, Doo and I had three of our own kids and we were living in Washington. When Brenda was a baby, my mommy and daddy left Butcher Holler, Kentucky, and moved to Wabash, Indiana. They hated having to leave Kentucky, but there was no work there. The coal mines had shut down and it was move or starve. When Brenda was only about five years old, our daddy died. It was very hard on my mommy. Later Mommy married Daddy's first cousin, Tommy Butcher, and went to work in a nursing home as an aide. When me and Brenda were younger, it was like we had nothing in common. I used to say we came from two different worlds. I grew up in the mountains in eastern Kentucky, and she was raised up north in what seemed to me like a big city. Now I know it was just a big town. I am glad that Brenda had

From left to right: Peggy Sue, Beth Ruth, Crystal Gayle, Loretta, Clara Webb, and Jay Lee

a better life than I did. She got to go to school and have a real childhood, with dances and movies...all things I didn't have in Butcher Holler.

When Brenda graduated from high school, she came to stay with me in Nashville. She, too—like me, Jay Lee, and Peggy Sue—wanted to sing, and I have to say she was really good. Doolittle and I really wanted to help her get started, so I started working with her. I made her, Peggy Sue, and me all matching dresses for the stage. I thought we were all so pretty up there in our outfits. I look at those pictures now and laugh...what was I *thinking*?!

The record companies already had a big artist named Brenda Lee, so we needed to find a new stage name for Brenda. I always liked the name Crystal and she did, too, so we changed her name to Crystal Gayle. It would be harder, we knew, for Crystal to make it in this business because of the success her sisters already had. Folks would be like, "Oh no, not another one." Ha! But Crystal was different, and we all knew it. I started writing songs for her and pushing her to the record companies. Me and Doo really got behind

her. We finally got her signed to her first record contract, and I wrote two songs for the record. Her first single, "I've Cried the Blue Right Out of My Eyes."

But I think people kept comparing her to me. She knew if she was going to make it she needed to be different. I always have said Crystal is more pop country than just country. In 1976 she recorded "Don't It Make My Brown Eyes Blue," and, man, she took off like a rocket. She married her hometown boyfriend, Bill Gotzimos. They are still married today and have two children. In the seventies and eighties Crystal and I were so busy we didn't get to see a lot of each other. But I was so proud of her. She made it on her own.

The other day, Patsy, my daughter, showed me an old film clip from a show called *Pop Goes Country*. Ralph Emery was the host. It was a clip from around 1981 and it had me, Jay Lee, Crystal, Peggy Sue, my son Ernest, and my mommy on it. We were all singing an old song my mommy had taught us called "The Titanic." Watching it, I thought to myself, *Boy, I know our mommy was really proud of all of us.*

"I've Cried the Blue Right Out of My Eyes"

RELEASE DATE 1978
ALBUM *I've Cried the Blue Right Out of My Eyes* (released by Crystal Gayle)

The reason I have put this song in my song book is I thought this story should be told. All of you know how country I write and how country I sing. And how country I *am*. At the time I wrote this, I was trying to get my little sister Crystal Gayle on the same label I was on, Decca Records. I knew she didn't sing real country, but she also wasn't too pop. I felt her place was down the middle of the road—country with a pop flavor to it because Crystal was

Loretta and Brenda Lee, 1979

105

raised in the city listening to a different kind of music, and I was raised in the mountains listening to the *Grand Ole Opry*. I have to say it was the hardest song I ever wrote because I wanted it to have a pop flavor. I arranged the song. I felt after I wrote it that maybe other writers could write better for Crystal than I could because I didn't want her sounding like me. I wanted her to have her own sound because I always knew she was great, and I wanted her to be even greater. And she is. Crystal, I'm proud to be your sister. I love you.

Oh, I've hurt enough for the both of
    us, since we said our good byes
And I've cried and cried until I've
    cried the blue right out of my
    eyes
If you hear a beat look down at
    your feet for that's where my
    heart lies
I should run and hide because I've
    cried the blue right out of my
    eyes

Now my eyes are gray the blues all
    washed away from tears I've cried
    for you
I need you close to me baby
    honestly I love you, you know
    that I do
Come on back again; don't say it's
    the end
Or don't you realize since you left
    my side darling I've cried the blue
    right out of my eyes

Now my eyes are gray the blues all
    washed away from the tears I've
    cried for you
I need you close to me baby
    honestly I love you, know that
    I do
Come on back again don't say it's
    the end
Or don't you realize since you left
    my side darling
I've cried the blue right out of my
    eyes

"Mama, It's Different This Time"

RELEASE DATE 1978
ALBUM *I've Cried the Blue Right Out of My Eyes* (released by Crystal Gayle)

Mama, Billy's not like all the rest,
Out of all the boys I've known, he's
    the best.
You said that I'm too young to love,
    and to cross him from my mind.
Oh but Mama, it's different this
    time.

Billy has a job after school,
He drives a car and the way he
    looks is cool,
The boy I thought I loved last week,
    he sure fed me a line
Oh but Mama, it's different this
    time.

You see this class ring that I wear,
He gave it to me today
I put it on this golden chain, and
    we're gonna marry someday.

The other girls all envy me, 'cause
they know Billy's mine.
And Mama, it's different this time.

"Sparklin' Look of Love"

RELEASE DATE 1978
ALBUM *I've Cried the Blue Right Out of My Eyes* (released by Crystal Gayle)

When I saw you my heart went
thumpety thump
Then you smiled at me, and my
head went bumpety bump
I knew then I was a goner, it wasn't
hard to realize
You put that sparklin' look of love
in my eyes.

I can hear the love birds singin'
tweedlee dee
And the feeling that I feel is fiddle
dee dee
Hello world I'm in love, and what a
sweet surprise
You put that sparklin' look of love
in my eyes

That look of love is in my eyes, as
far as I can see
And everything I touch turns to
love around me
You took the blue from my heart
and you placed it in the sky
You put that sparklin' look of love
in my eyes

That look of love is in my eyes as far
as I can see

And everything I touch turns to
love around me
You took the blue from my heart
and you placed it in the sky
You put that sparklin' look of love
in my eyes

"I Should Be Over You By Now"

WRITTEN WITH Theresa Ann Beaty
RELEASE DATE 1980
ALBUM *Loretta*

I've had time to learn to live again
And time enough for a broken
mind to mend
But time alone is not enough
somehow
'Cause I should be over you by now

I should be over you by now
I tried to love you more than I know
how
Just as our forevers had its end
When will gettin' over you begin
'Cause I should be over you by now

I have walked the road of my
mistakes
Stumblin' through the memories
we made
Feelin' so much hurt would never
heal
Or could it be you're feelin' what I
feel

'Cause I should be over you by now
I tried to love you more than I know
how

Gwyneth Paltrow, Loretta, and Sissy Spacek at the 2010 Country Music Awards

Just as our forevers had its end
When will gettin' over you begin
'Cause I should be over you by now

"Then You'll Be Free"

RELEASE DATE 1982
ALBUM *Making Love from Memory*

Oh, I've known for so long,
I barely manage to hang on,
But there's some reasons why I just
    can't let go.
It won't be long till the baby's gone,
Today she's here, tomorrow grown.
The ties that bind us will be
    behind us,
Then you'll be free.

Oh it's past my suffer time,
That hunger pain has made me lose
    my mind.

I've been starving for some love
    you gave away.
I'd like to make you pay by making
    you stay
Like giving you life and a day.
The ties that bind us will be
    behind us,
Then you'll be free.

Oh what you want is what you'll
    get,
Oh but I ain't ready to give it to you
    yet.
You love to party and the parties
    you love
And without the heartaches, you
    never think of.
It won't be long until they're gone.
Today they're here, tomorrow
    grown.
The ties that bind us will be
    behind us,
Then you'll be free.

"Smooth Talkin' Daddy"

WRITTEN WITH Sissy Spacek
RELEASE DATE 1983
ALBUM *Hanging Up My Heart*

Chorus:
Smooth talkin' daddy
You better quit your foolin' around
You've got a fast thinkin' mama
Fast thinkin' mama
So smooth talkin' daddy
Ain't got the time to get the jump
   on me, naw

You go love up her time
You done loved up all of mine
I ain't got nothin' left for you honey

Changed the locks on my door
Your key don't fit here no more
I got my bedroom changed round
And I'm ready

Chorus:
Smooth talkin' daddy
You better quit your foolin' around
You've got a fast thinkin' mama
Fast thinkin' mama
So smooth talkin' daddy
Ain't got the time to get the jump
   on me, naw

Tore all your pictures down
Threw out the clothes that I found
'Cause I'm cleaning my house out
   honey

Gonna get over you
By gettin' everything new
'Cause you've hurt me the last time
   honey

[Repeat chorus]

Set of *Coal Miner's Daughter*

"Wouldn't It Be Great"

RELEASE DATE 1985
ALBUM *Just a Woman*

I wrote "Wouldn't It Be Great" and recorded it on an album that Tammy Wynette and Dolly Parton and I did together called *Honky Tonk Angels*. This was a bittersweet time for me. I love both of these women. In fact, Tammy and I were very close friends. She was one of the only girls that I let get close to me since Patsy Cline died. But Doo was so sick when the girls wanted to record this, and my heart just wasn't there making this record.

All three of us, me, Tammy, and Dolly, were going through songs, picking out what we wanted to record together. I played them "Wouldn't It Be Great," and they both loved it. I love this song, too. I wrote it at the house we had in Nashville a few years before. My husband, as everybody knows, liked his whiskey. As with all alcoholics, the bottle takes over every part of their life. Even though me and Doo were alone in the house for the

Dolly, Mooney, and Loretta,
1990

first time in years and could spend time together with no hassles, he just wanted to drink. And he would—every day until he would pass out.

I was just sitting in my chair one night, watching him passed out on the sofa, and I thought to myself I no longer had Doo . . . the bottle did. But I prayed that one day that bottle would lose its hold on him and that I'd get him back.

I recorded this song not too long ago out at John Carter Cash's studio. He and Patsy have been recording a lot of old songs of mine as well as the new songs I've been writing. When I was singing it again, I thought how Doo was no longer with me, and it made me sad—the bottle won.

**Wouldn't it be fine if you could say
you love me just one time**

**With a sober mind
Wouldn't that be fine, now
wouldn't that be fine**

**Wouldn't it be great if you could
love me first and let the bottle
wait
Wouldn't that be great, now
wouldn't that be great**

**Wouldn't it be great, wouldn't that
be great
Throw the old glass crutch away
and watch it break
Wouldn't it be great, wouldn't that
be great
Lord, it's for our sake
Now wouldn't that be great**

**In the name of love what's a man
so great keep thinking of
What a man he was in the name of
love, in the name of love
Love went to waste when the sexy
lace wouldn't turn his face**

The bottle took my place love went
    to waste

Wouldn't it be great, wouldn't that
    be great
Throw the old glass crutch away
    and watch it break
Wouldn't it be great, wouldn't that
    be great
Lord, it's for our sake
Now wouldn't that be great

Wouldn't it be good and I know you
    could
If you just would

Wouldn't that be good
And you know you should

Wouldn't it be great, wouldn't that
    be great
Throw the old glass crutch away
    and watch it break
Wouldn't it be great, wouldn't that
    be great
Lord, it's for our sake
Now wouldn't that be great

Lord, it's for our sake
Now wouldn't that be great

Loretta, Dolly Parton, and
Tammy Wynette, 1993

"Adam's Rib"

RELEASE DATE 1985
ALBUM *Just a Woman*

Everybody knows I like to write songs for us girls, and "Adam's Rib" is one of those. It's a fun twist of a way to say, "Hey, we women have come a long way!" We sure have. I can't wait for the day a woman becomes president of the United States. I heard someone say somewhere that a country that keeps women down and doesn't let them have a say in running things still lives in mud houses. I loved that. It is so true. And I'm glad we don't live in mud houses anymore.

They say a woman was made to
please a man. Hey forget that
Leroy
If Adam was meant to play around
then he'd have made Eve a toy
A little windup doll that don't run
down and never gets a headache
like we do
The reason Adam didn't have a
little madam on the side
The good Lord didn't make him two

Chorus:
From Adam's rib to woman's lib
We've come a long way from
cookin' and rockin' the crib
This is my night out, don't know
what I'll do
The good Lord only knows what I'll
get into

Well, I won't go as far as some of
'em do
But hang in there girls, 'cause we
ain't through
The Lord made man, and man made
his woman to do what he wanted
her to

Hey, hey, girls, we're catchin' up
with him
Lord it's good for us and it's good
for them
It's from working hard and working
late
If there's lovin' on his mind, he'll
just have to wait

[Repeat chorus]

"Elzie Banks"

RELEASE DATE 1988
ALBUM *Who Was That Stranger*

This is a true story song. In Butcher Holler we had a one-room schoolhouse where we all went to school. But on Sunday it turned into our church. Elzie Banks was our pastor and a great one, too. Boy, I tell you, when he would get going he could really lay it on you. He told us like it was. Mommy taught all of us kids about the Lord and would read the Bible to us. But Elzie would Hell Fire and Brimstone you. He had all us kids so scared we would never do anything bad. Ha! Ole Elzie saved a lot of souls and spent his life working for the Lord. He was just a little country preacher. I believe God handpicks certain people to share His word and I know Elzie was one of them He chose. When I wrote "Elzie Banks" it was my way of thanking him for sharing the Lord with all of us in Butcher Holler.

There's an old-time preacher
    named Elzie Banks
And he tells you like it is.
He said you can't be good if you're
    a little bit bad
'Cause the devil knows you're his.
And when he preaches about fire
    and brimstone
You can almost see the flames
When he says you'll walk them
    golden streets
Ten thousand angels sing.

He'll break ice on the river in the
    middle of the wintertime
And say come on sister wade right
    in the water's mighty fine
He'll raise one hand toward the
    heaven and then he'd say let's
    pray
Come on Lord let's show this world
    we're gonna drown the old devil
    today.

And we'll sing
Come on children let your
    little light shine, high from a
    mountaintop
We'll get a kick outa watchin' the
    devil settin' them stumbling
    blocks

This world's the devil's playground
    and I hate like the devil to say
He's the hardest worker in this
    world, he works twenty-five
    hours a day.

Preacher Elzie keep on a preachin',
    you never let your people down
I miss the old camp meetin' time
    and dinner on the ground
He's an old-time country preacher
    he preaches the gospel free
The mountain people need him and
    they love him just like me.

Lord I wouldn't be caught dead
    without my Jesus to hold on to
If you don't know your Lord today,
    tomorrow He won't know you
Don't get me wrong I believe in
    givin' I strongly believe in faithin'
Are the TV preachers losin' souls for
    the bank accounts they're savin'

And we'll sing
Come on children let your
    little light shine, high from a
    mountaintop
We'll get a kick outa watchin' the
    devil settin' them stumbling
    blocks
This world's the devil's playground
    and I hate like the devil to say
He's the hardest worker in this
    world, he works twenty-five
    hours a day.

"Mountain Climber"

RELEASE DATE 1988
ALBUM *Who Was That Stranger*

My mommy used to say I wasn't afraid of nothing. To tell me I couldn't do something was like daring me to do it. If you said to me, "You can't," I was gonna show you I could!

I've always been a hard worker, and with hard work you can do whatever you set your mind to. That is how I have lived my life. I'm a Mountain Climber. The higher the mountain, the better I like 'em.

Everybody's gotta start somewhere
Most wanna start at the top
When they fail it ain't the fall that
  hurts
Lord it's the sudden stop
I've got a lot of ambition
And I love competition
I'll give it all a try
And I'll do or die
'Cause I'm a mountain climber
Yeah I'm a mountain climber
The higher the mountain the better
  I like 'em

When I got a dream I go for it
When a dream comes true I'll
  know it
A quitter is a loser
A winner never quits
And I never stop till I get to the top
'Cause I'm a mountain climber
Well I wake every morning
And I'm rarin' to go
At the bottom of a brand-new hill
I'm like a race horse
Ready to run
I just can't stand still
I love to be in action
I like the feel of satisfaction
I'm not satisfied till I see the other
  side
'Cause I'm a mountain climber
Yeah I'm a mountain climber
The higher the mountain the better
  I like 'em
When I got a dream I go for it
When a dream comes true I'll
  know it
A quitter is a loser
A winner never quits
And I never stop till I get to the top
'Cause I'm a mountain climber
No I never stop till I get to the top
'Cause I'm a mountain climber

Country in My Genes

In 1999 I started recording an album called *Country in My Genes*. It was the first time I had recorded a solo record in over a decade, and I picked a producer named Randy Scruggs. His daddy is Earl Scruggs from Flatt and Scruggs. They were big stars when I first came to Nashville. Randy has really made a name for himself on his own. He is not only a great producer, he's also a great musician like his daddy. I had started tryin' to write songs again for this new record. I really think it's easier to write when you have something to write for. I wrote two songs for this album: "God's Country" and "I Can't Hear the Music." I'm so glad that Randy and I got to work together. I still use him to come play guitar for me in the studio. Every time I record I tell myself, "If Randy Scruggs ain't playin' I ain't comin'!"

"I Can't Hear the Music"

WRITTEN WITH Kendal Franceschi and Jamie Johannes Soderlund
RELEASE DATE 2000
ALBUM *Still Country*

I cowrote this song with Kendal Franceschi and Jamie Johannes Soderlund. He wrote for my publishing company, Coal Miners Music. This is a very special song. I only sang it live one time and cried through the whole song.

The idea for this song came from my late husband, Doo. Doolittle was my biggest fan and if ya'll know anything about my life, then ya'll know what Doo meant to me. He was and will always be my everything. Doo loved my singing and he thought every song I wrote was a hit. Ha! He would help me pick out what songs I was going to record for all my albums. Doo had a great ear for good songs, but as much as he loved music, bless his heart, he couldn't sing a lick! That's right. And he was even worse off tune when he whistled! But he was great at coming up with ideas or titles for songs. He would just drive around in his jeep on our ranch in Hurricane Mills and have his tape recorder, and when he thought of a line or a title he would record it and play them all for me when I came home off the road.

In 1993 Doolittle got real sick. He had to have open heart surgery. But Doo was a real bad diabetic, and diabetes is one of the worst diseases anybody could have. I do all I can do to help find a cure for diabetes.

Anyway . . . Doo had his open heart surgery in a hospital in Springfield, Missouri. We had bought a theater there and were staying there doing two shows a day for about a year when he got sick. The surgery went great, and we thought Doo was going to be fine. But one day about a week and a half after the heart operation, Doo was sitting up in the bed, and he coughed and his chest just opened up. Because of the diabetes he was not healing from the inside. Then it was just one problem after another. We spent months in that Springfield hos-

pital. Finally, we got to bring Doo back home to the ranch in Hurricane Mills. He was alive but dying little by little every day. I stopped working, stopped everything, and stayed by Doo's side twenty-four hours a day taking care of him.

Even when Doo was sick he still loved to listen to music. He loved George Jones, Patsy Cline, Tammy Wynette, and, of course, me. In early 1996, Doolittle was losing his battle with diabetes. He was in so much pain. I would try everything I could think of to lift his spirits and try to get his mind off the pain. So I put on one of my albums, and I was playing it, sitting beside him on the bed, rubbing his head, when he looked at me and said, "Honey, I can't hear the music anymore." Well, I thought he wanted me to turn it up, so I did. Then he said, "No, I mean I can't hear the music anymore," and a tear rolled down his face. My heart broke in a million pieces.

My husband passed away on August 22, 1996. I wrote this song for Doolittle, and I know he's in heaven listening to music again, with ears wide open.

He showed me there was more to
   me when I thought I had nothing
   else to give
God knows he wasn't perfect, ah,
   but then again, nobody is.

He always told me the truth no
   matter how hard it was to hear
When he said, "I believe in you"
   that was music to my ears.

Oh, each word is like a note, like a
   beautiful tune
The kind that inspires and helps me
   get through
Ah, if I said I can't, he'd say "you
   can."
He was my toughest critic, ah, my
   biggest fan.

Now he's gone to a distant shore
And I can't hear the music anymore.

Sometimes late at night I forget
   that he's not lying next to me.

He may be out of sight, but out
   of mind is something he won't
   ever be.

Things that he said to me are still
   ringing out loud and clear
When he said "I love you baby,"
   that was music to my ears.

Oh, each word is like a note, like a
   beautiful tune
The kind that inspires and helps
   you get through
Ah, if I said I can't, he'd say "you
   can."
He was my toughest critic, ah, my
   biggest fan.

Now he's gone to a distant shore
And I can't hear the music anymore.

I can't hear the music.

"God's Country"

RELEASE DATE 2000
ALBUM *Still Country*

Lord knows, I couldn't tell you how long it took me to write or rewrite this song...and I don't know why. It's just a funny little mountain song. But I must have pieces of it in every notepad I had! I just wrote bits and pieces whenever something came to me. I still sing this sometimes in my live shows. When my twins Patsy and Peggy work on the road with me, I get them to come out onstage and we all sing it together.

**Well I was borned in old Kentucky
In them hills where folks are lucky
From a coal miner's daughter right
to a coal miner's wife**

**Well the mountain folks love the
mountains
White lightning flowed like the
fountains
On a Sunday morning you can hear
all the good folks singin'**

**It's God's country in these hills He
walks
And in the middle of the night you
can hear Him talk
It's the closest place to heaven that
I know**

**If you wanna get to heaven get
your road map out
It's called the Bible—if you have
one doubt
I guess my friends, you must be on
the wrong route.**

**Well I miss the old camp meeting
time and dinner on the ground
What I miss most is everything like
all the country sounds
Like the lonesome sound of the
whip-poor-will sang me to sleep
every night
And the whistle of the old freight
train before daylight.**

**Chorus:
It's God's country in these hills He
walks
And in the middle of the night you
can hear Him talk
It's the closest place to heaven that
I know
If you wanna go to heaven get your
road map out
It's called the Bible—if you have
one doubt
I guess my friends, you must be on
the wrong route.**

**[Repeat chorus]
And my old Kentucky home's far
away.**

Van Lear Rose project

Sometimes people just come into your life that you would never expect. That's what Jack White did. Who would have ever thought I would have a record with a rock and roller from Detroit? Not me. But I am sure glad I did.

Jack grew up in Detroit, Michigan. He was from a big family, just like me. He went to the movie theaters and saw my movie *Coal Miner's Daughter*. He said it changed his life. He became a big fan of my songs and songwriting. He and Meg even dedicated their White Stripes record to me (*White Blood Cells*). They wrote me a letter and sent me the record. Well, I have to say I had never heard of them. But I loved the CD. My manager at the time, Nancy Russell, called and set up a day

Loretta and Jack White at the Grammys, 2005

for Jack and Meg to come see me at my ranch in Hurricane Mills. I made them dinner—chicken and dumplings and my homemade bread. Jack still says that it was the best bread he ever ate. I gave little Meg one of my old stage dresses to wear. Bless her heart, she just cried. Meg is so sweet. I had been telling Patsy I wanted to start recording and make another record soon. So I had all my songs out, trying to get them together and sort through them, when Nancy called me and asked if I would plan a show in New York with Jack and Meg. I said, "Sure."

What fun we had. If ya'll ain't never seen Jack and Meg, you should. It's just little Meg on drums and Jack. Let me tell you that boy can sing and play his guitar. But it's rock and roll, not country. I told Jack I was getting ready to record my songs. He said he'd love to work with me on doing that.

Nancy Russell set it up, and the rest is history. The album is called *Van Lear Rose,* and Jack recorded fifteen songs. He only wanted to record songs I had written. I had only done that one time before, on my very first record. We recorded in this old house in east Nashville. I swear I thought that house was going to fall in around us. Jack picked out the players and what songs he wanted, and I sang them. We recorded the whole dang record in two weeks. I only got to sing the songs one or two times. Every time I would sing something, Jack would say, "I love it." I thought Jack was like a young Owen Bradley. He wants you to just be who you are and do what you do. I am telling you he is great. I love him so much. We are really great friends now.

And we won two Grammys for *Van Lear Rose*!

"Family Tree"

RELEASE DATE 2004
ALBUM *Van Lear Rose*

"Family Tree" is one of those songs that I wrote in five minutes. It's about another woman who has taken my husband away and has burnt down our family tree. Now, there was never a woman who was woman enough to take my man away, but I love to write these kinds of songs. And let me tell you, when I am writing them I still get so mad. I used to start hollering at Doolittle even though he hadn't done anything! He would say, "Loretta, it's just a song. You have gone crazy!"

Crazy or not, I love these kinds of songs, and they are real. Even if they're not real, if you know what I mean. No one ever burned down my family tree, but a lot of women tried, that's for sure.

I have a line in the song: *I brought along his old dog Charlie and the bills that's overdue.* My husband and I had an old dog named Henry, but that didn't sound as good as Charlie. Haha!

**Woman, you don't know me, but
    you can bet that I know you
Everybody in this whole darn town
    knows you too
I brought along our little babies,
    'cause I wanted them to see
The woman that's burnin' down our
    family tree**

The Lynn family, 1994

No I didn't come to fight
If he was a better man I might
But I wouldn't dirty my hands on
    trash like you, no
Bring out the babies' daddy, that's
    who they've come to see
Not the woman that's burnin' down
    our family tree

Their daddy once was a good man,
    until he ran into trash like you
Take a look at the baby's face and
    tell me who loves who
I brought along his old dog Charlie
    and the bills that's overdue
The job you're workin' . . . Lord, we
    need money, too

No I didn't come to fight
If he was a better man I might
But I wouldn't dirty my hands on
    trash like you, no
Bring out the babies' daddy, that's
    who they've come to see
Not the woman that's burnin' down
    our family tree
No not the woman that's burnin'
    down our family tree

"God Makes No Mistakes"

RELEASE DATE 2004
ALBUM *Van Lear Rose*

I love how me and Jack recorded this
song. I sang a little bit of this song to
him not long after we met, and he
really liked it. There are so many bad

things in this world that sometimes it
makes us all ask the question: "Why?"
Why do people we love die too soon?
Why are people out there hungry? So
many things . . . why why why?! But
for me I believe there is a reason why
everything happens the way it does,
even if it hurts, and I know that God
makes no mistakes.

Why, I've heard people say
Why is this tree bent
Why they don't have God enough
    to know
That's the way that it was meant
Why is this little baby born
All twisted and out of shape
We're not to question what He
    does
God makes no mistakes.

Why, I've heard people say
Why is my child blind
Why is that old drunk still livin'
When a daddy like mine is dyin'
Our Blessed Father gives us life
Has the power to take it away
There's no reason for what He does
God makes no mistakes.

Why, I've heard people say
God cannot be alive
And all the things people say
Has to be a lie
When they're down and out
And they need a hand
And their very soul's at stake
If they'll just call on Him and just
    believe
God makes no mistakes.

"High on a Mountain Top"

WRITTEN WITH Patsy Lynn Russell
RELEASE DATE 2004
ALBUM *Van Lear Rose*

High on a mountain top
We live, we love, and we laugh a lot
Folks up here know what they got
High on a mountain top
High on a mountain top

Chorus:
Where the rest of the world's like a
    little bitty spot
I ain't comin' down no never I'm not
High on a mountain top
High on a mountain top

Where I come from the mountain
    flowers grow wild
The blue grass sways like it's goin'
    out of style
God fearin' people simple and real
'Cause up on the ridge folks that's
    the deal

Well my daddy worked down in the
    dark coal mine
Shovelin' that coal one shovel at a
    time
Never made a lot of money didn't
    have much
But we're high on life and rich in
    love

High on a mountain top
We live, we love, and we laugh a lot
Folks up here know what they got
High on a mountain top
High on a mountain top

[Repeat chorus]
Well down in the holler lived my
    uncle Joe
He'd pull out his fiddle and rosin his
    bow
We'd all sing and dance
And we ain't gonna stop
When the moonshine flows behind
    every rock

High on a mountain top
We live, we love, and we laugh a lot
Folks up here know what they got
High on a mountain top
High on a mountain top

[Repeat chorus]
Well we lay on our backs and we
    count the stars
'Cause up here folks heaven's not
    that far

High on a mountain top
We live, we love, and we laugh a lot
Folks up here know what they got
High on a mountain top
High on a mountain top

[Repeat chorus]
High on a mountain top
High on a mountain top

Have Mursey

Have mursey on me babe
Im down upon my knees
Have mursey on me babe
I'll go just as you please.
you no that I love you I'll
But no one else shove her
Have Mercy — — — —

Ill you no I no just how to love
you. I'll learn what I don't no
know you. you no I no just
how to love you. and Im
ready how to show you,

I no how to touch and
kiss you baby. I no how you
are. and how you fell, Tell me
what you want. and how you
fell, I move in for the kill
Have mursy — —

Have Mursey on me baby. Im
down upon my knee,
you no I no just how to
love you. and Im ready now
show you, Have mursey on
me baby.

you showed me How to love you
by your self. Dont go showing
some one else, Baby I

"Have Mercy"

RELEASE DATE 2004
ALBUM *Van Lear Rose*

I get so tickled every time I hear this song on this record. It's me trying to sing rock and roll—and friends, it was fun.

"Have Mercy" was a song I played for Jack, and he grabbed his guitar and started playing this rock-and-roll beat, and we just went with it. I remember Jack being in the vocal room with me when I started singing this to the track he had laid down. He had this big grin on his face. He was sayin', "Get with it, Loretta," and boy, I did.

Have mercy on me baby
I'm down upon my knees
Have mercy on me baby
I'll do just as you please
Well you know that I love you
I'll put no one else above you
Have mercy on me baby, have
   mercy

Have mercy on me baby
Please have a little heart

Have mercy on me baby
You're tearing me apart
The way that you do me
You know you done got to me
Have mercy on me baby, have
   mercy

She's got you hypnotized
And your brain is paralyzed
You know she's only playing with
   you
Like a puppet on a string
Remember just one thing
She can't love you like I do, no

Have mercy on me baby
Please give this heart a break
Have mercy on me baby
I'll do just what it takes
You know you won't regret it
So hey there now I said it
Have mercy on me baby, have
   mercy

Have mercy
Have mercy on me
Have mercy on me baby
Have mercy on me
Have mercy on me baby
Please have mercy on me

"Little Red Shoes"

WRITTEN WITH John Anthony White
RELEASE DATE 2004
ALBUM *Van Lear Rose*

Jack White had this melody track, and he and I were talking about trying to write a song together to this melody. So we're sitting in the studio listening and talking. Jack was having them play the track over and over for me so I maybe could think of a song title or words. But he pulled a fast one on me! I started telling him a story about when I was a little girl and my daddy and mommy had saved up enough money and they bought me a pair of little red shoes. They were the prettiest things I ever saw. That same year I got really sick, and the town doctor told Mommy I might die, and I almost did. My mommy put my little red shoes away thinking I would never get to wear them.

Well, I did get better and I did wear those shoes, and how I loved them! I was just sitting and talking to Jack, telling him all about this. I didn't know he was taping me. When we were done he said, "Well, there's the song!"

I said, "What?"

He played it back to me, and I said, "Are you kidding me?"

He said, "No," and he meant it.

Funny thing is a lot of people have told me how much they love that track of me just talking to Jack's music.

I was eleven months old, I was just
    startin' to walk
And Daddy always kept a big stick
    behind the door
Just in case somebody was to
    come in
That was drunk on moonshine

You know and Daddy had to do
    something about it
Anyway, this woman, we called her
    old Aunt Boyd
She come in and she was telling
    Mommy about her
Uh, husband, she thinks is
    going out with this woman in
    Paintsville

So she reared back with that big
    stick
Showing Mommy how she was
    going
To hit this woman in the head
    with it
And when she went back with it,
    she hit me in the head

And Mommy said, I cried for five
    days
And she said I, that fifth night
I had a great big knot that
    showed up
Right in the middle of my forehead

And, you know, the only thing I
    remember

I don't remember no pain, but I just
    remember Mommy
And Daddy carrying me in this old
    quilt
That Mommy had made out of
    overalls

The knots kept getting bigger and
    bigger
So she took me to the doctor
And that stuff called mesitor,
    something like that
Mommy said it made both ears flat
    to my face
And I ain't got very big ears

And then told Mommy I was going
    to die
And that happened like four times
So I didn't walk 'til I was almost five
It was kind of a mess

Oh I forgot about the shoes
Well, shoot, I hadn't never had a
    pair of shoes
And Mommy took me to the
    hospital
You know, to see what that was

They couldn't do something
So they wouldn't keep me
Because Mommy and Daddy didn't
    have no money
They just tell 'em to take me home
    and let me die
You know because there wasn't
    nothing they could do
About that kind of a disease, I
    guess

And, um, Mommy told Daddy, says,
Ted take her down the street
You carry her down the street and
    she said
Let me try this store here
And Mommy went in and told them
    the story that I was dying

That she had to carry me twelve
    miles to town
And twelve miles back and I had no
    shoes
The place I think it was Murphy's
    five and ten and
They're still in Paintsville, Kentucky

And I think they told Mommy
They wasn't in business to give
    shoes away
Mommy told Daddy, says, Carry
    Loretta on down a little farther
Said, and let me stop in another
    store

And Mommy went right back to the
    same store
When the guy's back was turned
    she stole these little red shoes
And I remember on the big old
    bridge that went across the river
It went way up high and was . . .

I've always been scared of that
    bridge
That took me across the big Sandy
    River
Mommy pulled them out from
    under
That yellow jacket that she was
    wearing

And she was putting them red
    shoes on me
And I thought them was the
    prettiest thing I ever saw in my
    life
And Daddy started crying and I
    wondered why
And he said, Clerie, we're not going
    to make it home

And Mommy put the shoes on me
    and Daddy took off running
And run all the way ahead to
    Butcher Holler with me
And Mommy never had a chance to
    carry me any farther
And that's almost twelve miles that
    Daddy run with me

But Daddy knew that the cops was
    going to get us
He left Mommy standing and he
    took off in a dead run
I remember him running but I didn't
    know what for
And I remember asking Mommy,
    Mommy, why is Daddy running?

I remember her hollering, to put
    your little red shoes away
Honey, when you get home. Can
    you believe that?
So I wrote a song called "Put My
    Little Red Shoes Away"
You know, they're my little red
    shoes
And I don't want 'em to get to be
    dirty.

"Miss Being Mrs."

WRITTEN WITH Philip Russell and
Maggie Vaughn
RELEASE DATE 2004
ALBUM *Van Lear Rose*

There were very few girl songwriters in the sixties. It sure was a
man's world. Nothing against men
writers—Lord knows there were some
great ones. But I always felt that only
a woman really knows how a woman
feels about things. I couldn't understand why there weren't more girls
out there writing songs. The great
ones like Cindy Walker and Betty Sue
Petty were few and far between. One
of the first girls that I cowrote with
was a gal named Maggie Vaughn.

Maggie was so much fun to write
with and just to be around. She made
everyone laugh all the time. Maggie
was a great lyric writer. She didn't
really write a melody. She would read
you her song lyric like a poem, and I
would jump in there and start singing a melody. We wrote a few songs
together, one Ernest Tubb cowrote
called "Bartender" and a song called
"L.O.V.E." We started a lot of songs
together, but we never finished most
of 'em. Doolittle said we girls just
talked more than we worked...and
we did.

I lost touch with Maggie in the
seventies. I was working three hun-

dred days a year. But I thought of her from time to time, always saying I needed to call her. In 2004 when Jack White and I were deciding on what songs to record for the *Van Lear Rose* album, I was going through all my old songs, stacks of old papers with an idea here and a line or two there, on everything from hotel stationery to napkins, when I saw a verse and part of a title called "Miss Being Mrs."

I wrote so many songs I don't even remember most of them, even my hits. I called my son-in-law, Philip Russell, who's also a great songwriter, and he and I finished the song and Jack recorded it. After the album came out, Maggie called the office and talked to Patsy and told her, "Hey, me and your momma started that song when you were just a baby." Patsy gave Maggie my number and she called me. Both of us laughed our heads off. I told her, "Well, heck, Maggie, I can't remember from one day to the next half the time much less a song forty years ago."

Of course, we called BMI and had her added to the song as a writer.

Things happen for a reason, I always say, and finding that song and recording it all those years later brought me and Maggie back together again. Now we can write more. This was the first single off the *Van Lear Rose* record. We shot the video in my plantation home in Hurricane Mills. It was nominated in the Best Country Song category at the Grammys, and it should have won.

I lie here all alone
In my bed of memories
I'm dreamin' of your sweet kiss
Oh, how you loved on me
I can almost feel you with me
Here in this blue moonlight
Oh, I miss being Mrs. tonight.

Like so many other hearts
Mine wanted to be free
I've been held here every day
Since you've been away from me
My reflection in the mirror
It's such a hurtful sight
Oh, I miss being Mrs. tonight.

Oh, I miss being Mrs. tonight
Oh, and how I loved them loving
** arms**
That once held me so tight
I took off my wedding band
And put it on my right hand
I miss being Mrs. tonight.

Oh, I miss being Mrs. tonight
Oh, and how I loved them loving
** arms**
That once held me so tight
I took off my wedding band
And put it on my right hand
I miss being Mrs. tonight.

Oh, I miss being Mrs. tonight.

Best Western

Midway Motor Lodge
"FEATURING THE HOFFMAN HOUSE RESTAURANT"
On The Black River • 1835 Rose Street
LA CROSSE, WISCONSIN 54601
(608) 784-8865

Portland Oregon + Slow Gin Fiz it
that ain,t Come then Tell me what is
Ho, Ho. Ho Bar Made Ally dont be So Slow
Bring us one drink tor Now. and make us
to Move to 90, Ho,

in a booth in a corner with the lights he.S
~~Mary in~~ in fort. and I'm movin it Slow
Ho, Yeon, I looped up at him, ~~And She~~
~~right here that~~, ul New right then that
ul were Home free in Orgen,

That slow Gin fiz a working mighty fast. when
you drink it by the Pitch + not By a glass Ho,
Nextt day we New last night got so drunk
at side. ftor the night sobering up, ul
Had that look ot Sotshide'

"Portland, Oregon"

RELEASE DATE 2004
ALBUM *Van Lear Rose*

I have to tell ya'll, when me and Jack recorded this song it was late at night, and I went in and sang the song and left. The next day I came back to the studio, and Eric the engineer was playing me and Jack back some of the songs we'd been singing. Well, "Portland, Oregon" came on, and I was just listening and all the sudden I heard someone else singing with me. I said, "Lord have mercy, who *is* that?"

Jack, who is really shy, put his head down and smiled and said, "That's me."

I gave him a big hug and said, "I love it." And I do.

I can't tell you when I started this song, but I have worked and worked on it for years. It's one of those songs that's just plain fun. Now, I don't drink at all, but I always heard that sloe gin fizz is a good drink, and it will get you drunk mighty fast. Ha! Me and Jack went to Memphis and shot a music video for this song. We filmed it in this old tavern. They said it was a famous place, and many years ago it was a brothel. Jack knows what he wants to do not only in music but in videos as well, so I just went with it. It was voted one of the best videos on CMT, I

think. All the players on the record are in the video. Patrick, the drummer, even had "Loretta Lynn" painted on his drums. That was so sweet.

Even Jack's friends, the boy and the redheaded girl who have a band of their own, Blanche, were in the video. They have done some shows with me as well. And my daughter Patsy begged her way into the video, too. She is sitting at the bar. That girl . . .

**Well, Portland, Oregon, and sloe
   gin fizz
If that ain't love, then tell me what
   is, uh huh, uh huh
Well I lost my heart, it didn't take
   no time
But that ain't all, I lost my mind in
   Oregon**

**In a booth in the corner with the
   lights down low
I was movin' in fast, she was takin'
   it slow uh huh, uh huh
Well, I looked at him and caught
   him lookin' at me
I knew right then we were playin'
   free in Oregon**

**Next day, we knew last night got
   drunk
But we loved enough for the both
   of us, uh huh, uh huh
In the morning when the night had
   sobered up
It was much too late for the both of
   us in Oregon**

Well, sloe gin fizz works mighty
    fast
When you drink it by the pitcher
    and not by the glass uh huh, uh
    huh
Hey bartender, before you close
Pour us one more drink and a
    pitcher to go

And a pitcher to go
(and a pitcher to go)
And a pitcher to go
(and a pitcher to go)

And a pitcher to go
(and a pitcher to go)
Yeah

"Mrs. Leroy Brown"

RELEASE DATE 2004
ALBUM *Van Lear Rose*

I laugh every time I hear this cut off *Van Lear Rose*. We really rocked it up! I told ya'll before how, when I am writing, I really feel the song. Well, this is a great example.

I was at my ranch in Hurricane Mills, and it was pretty early in the morning, and I would strum my guitar a little and come up with a new line or two, and I guess I was really getting into it and singing really loud. I was on the lines where I've done pulled up my limo at the old honky tonk where my husband was with another woman, and I'm singing of what all I'm gonna do to this old gal when I walk in. I had worked myself up so much I was yelling, saying, "I'm gonna grab her by her ponytail and sling her round and round," when in comes my assistant, Tim Cobb. He came running in out of breath sayin', "Loretta, are you okay?!"

I stopped and said, "Yes, why?"

He said that I'd scared him to death because it sounded like I was yelling at the top of my lungs. I told him I was. I was whippin' the old gal at the bar who was trying to take my ole man.

Then he just shook his head and

turned around and walked out of the room.

And I just started whippin' that old gal some more. Haha!

I've been in and out of every honky tonk in town
And I'm almost drunk from the drinks that I've turned down,
Well, you told me you'd be happy bouncin' babies on your knee
While I sit at home alone and I've been bouncin' three.
Yeah, and I'm tired of it too.

I'm gonna call myself a long pink limousine
Yeah, believe it or not it's the prettiest thing I think I've ever seen.
There's a big bar in the corner and a TV on the side
This baby's sixty feet long and forty feet wide.

Chorus:
Hey driver pull this car, buddy, right inside the bar
Take it on back to the big ol' blonde that thinks she's a movie star.
I'm gonna grab her by her phony ponytail
I'm gonna sling her around and around
When she wakes up she'll know she met up with mad Mrs. Leroy Brown.

Well the smoke's so doggone thick
You could cut it with a knife

And the music's so loud you can hear the same line twice.
Hey Leroy Brown, how do you like my big ol' pink limo
I just drawed all your money out of the bank today
Honey, you don't have no mo'.

I'm gonna call myself a long pink limousine
Yeah, believe it or not it's the prettiest thing I think I've ever seen.
There's a big bar in the corner and a TV on the side.
This baby's sixty feet long and forty feet wide.

[Repeat chorus]

137

"This Old House"

RELEASE DATE 2004
ALBUM *Van Lear Rose*

If you have seen my movie *Coal Miner's Daughter,* you saw my home in it. It's a big old white plantation house, and it's over three hundred years old. Doo and I bought the house and twelve hundred acres around it back in the early sixties. This was the only home we really lived in. We raised our kids there.

We worked so hard for years fixing up that house. Doo would say, "Loretta, we could have built twenty houses in downtown Nashville for what we spent fixing that house up!"

But Doo knew I loved it so much.

Mooney and Loretta at home, late 1980s

We had six kids, and Gloria, who helped with our kids, lived there, too. So really we needed that big house. But when my twin daughter Peggy, who was the last to leave home, got married, the house was empty. Doo called me out on the road and said, "Honey, I don't want to live in this big house alone." I must have cried for a year. But me and Doo built a smaller house right behind that house. He did that so I could stay close. We left everything in our plantation home just like it was when we all lived there. We even left all the ghosts as well!!!

We opened the house up for people to take tours in it in the late eighties and people still go through today. Sometimes when I am not on the road and I walk over to that home and just look around, I can close my eyes and still hear the kids laughing and Doolittle carrying on. It will always be my home. It will always be our real family home.

1, 2, 3 . . .

Oh if this old house could talk,
What a story it would tell
It would tell about the good times
And the bad times as well

It would tell about the love that lived,
And died inside these walls
And the footsteps,
Runnin' up and down the hall

Oh if this old house could talk,
It would break my heart in two
I couldn't stand to be reminded
Of all the things we used to do

There's no love in this old house no more,
So I got it up for sale
Why if this old house could talk
What a story it would tell

Oh if this old house could talk,
I know what it would say
I'm as lonesome as you are
And I feel more empty everyday

I even miss the babies
Who built me up to feel this way
Why if this old house could talk,
Lord I know what it would say

Yeah if this old house could talk,
What a story it would tell
We'll build this home together
And with love we drove each nail

Take me in your arms and hold me,
'Cause we've been apart too long
Why if this old house could talk,
All it would say is welcome home

"Trouble on the Line"

WRITTEN WITH O. V. Lynn
RELEASE DATE 2004
ALBUM *Van Lear Rose*

Doo would always try and come up with song ideas for me.

Now, Doo could do anything, fix any truck, drive bulldozers, break horses, you name it. But he could not sing a lick!

We'd be driving around with our twins and Doo would start singing as loud as he could and the babies would start hollerin': "Mommy, make Daddy stop!" But every now and then Doo would have a great idea for a song. I would always call home from the road to talk to Doo and the kids. I had this phone put in my bus so I could call them anytime I wanted to. But back then phone service was not very good and we always got disconnected. That was how Doo came up with the title for this song. But I was gone so much back in them days that it wasn't just phone service that was disconnected—it was a hard time for my relationship with Doo as well.

I can't understand a word you're
** sayin'**
We've got a bad connection on our
** minds**
Communication's one thing we
** never seem to find**
Oh Lord I'm sorry, but there's
** trouble on the line**

All I get is static when we're talkin'
You say my line is out of order all
** the time**
We have nothin' left in common
Your thoughts are not like mine
Oh Lord I'm sorry, but there's
** trouble on the line**

There's trouble on the line
From your heart to mine
Oh Lord I'm sorry but we're not
** gettin' through**

The storm keeps gettin' worse
Lord, we might as well quit tryin'
Oh Lord I'm sorry, but there's
** trouble on the line**
Oh Lord I'm sorry, but there's
** trouble on the line**

"Van Lear Rose"

WRITTEN WITH Patsy Lynn Russell
RELEASE DATE 2004
ALBUM *Van Lear Rose*

"Van Lear Rose" is a song about my mommy. Mommy was part Cherokee Indian. She was so pretty, with beautiful black hair that just curled, and the loveliest skin. When I was little I wanted to look just like her, but I never could be as pretty as my mommy.

Van Lear is the town that Butcher Holler is in. Butcher Holler is what ya'll might call a street. We didn't have streets, we had hollers.

I think this was the very first song I showed Jack. Patsy and I had started writing this song about the time I met him. I was thinking of my mommy, and Patsy said she was thinking of me. When we finished the record and were trying to think of what to call it, Nancy Russell said it should be called *Van Lear Rose*. Roses are my favorite flower.

One of my fondest memories
Was sittin' on my daddy's knee
Listenin' to the stories that he told
He'd pull out that old photograph
Like a treasured memory from the
** past**
And say child
This here's the Van Lear Rose

Oh how it would bring a smile
When he talked about her big blue
   eyes
And how her beauty ran down to
   her soul
She'd walk across the coal miner's
   yard

Them miners would yell loud and
   hard
And they'd dream of who would
   hold
The Van Lear Rose

She was the belle of Johnson
    Country
Ohio River to Big Sandy
A beauty to behold like a
    diamond in the coal
All the miners they would gather
    'round
Talk about the man that came to
    town
Right under their nose
Stole the heart of the Van Lear Rose

Now the Van Lear Rose could've
    had her pick
And all the fellers figured rich
Until this poor boy caught her eye
His buddies would all laugh and say
You're dreamin' boy she'll never
    look your way
You'll never ever hold the Van Lear
    Rose

She was the belle of Johnson
    Country
Ohio River to Big Sandy
A beauty to behold like a diamond
    in the coal
All the miners they would gather
    'round
Talk about the man that came to
    town
Right under their nose
Stole the heart of the Van Lear Rose

Then one night in mid-July
Underneath that ol' blue Kentucky
    sky
Well, that poor boy won that
    beauty's heart
Then my daddy would look at my
    Mommy and smile

As he brushed the hair back from
    my eyes and he'd say your mama
    she's the Van Lear Rose

She was the belle of Johnson
    Country
Ohio River to Big Sandy
A beauty to behold like a diamond
    in the coal
All the miners they would gather
    'round
Talk about the man who came to
    town
Right under their nose
Stole the heart of the Van Lear Rose

Right under their nose
Stole the heart of the Van Lear
    Rose.

"Women's Prison"

WRITTEN WITH Patsy Lynn Russell
RELEASE DATE 2004
ALBUM *Van Lear Rose*

Johnny Cash, Merle...well, a lot of singers and songwriters sang and wrote about prison. But I never heard a woman sing or write about one, so I thought it was about time. I don't know when I started the idea for this song, but I had this verse and a little chorus on a piece of paper in a stack of songs of mine. I had taken a bunch of my tablets of songs and titles out on the road with me to look through. Patsy rides the bus with me and was looking at my songs, trying to help me pick out a few. One morning, she came to the back of the bus with this old piece of paper and said, "Momma, what is this song?" I looked at it and said, "It's about a woman who's on death row for killing her cheating husband." She asked me to sing a little bit of it for her. So I made up a melody after a minute or two and sang some of what I wrote. She stood there and had the funniest look on her face. I said, "Honey, it ain't very good." Patsy is my biggest fan—she loves everything I do, even when it's so bad. She said, "Well, Momma, I think it's great!" So we finished it and Jack White loved it, too. I have to say it wound up bein' one of my favorite songs on the record.

I'm in a women's prison with bars
   all around
I caught my darlin' cheatin' that's
   when I shot him down
I caught him in a honky tonk with a
   girl I used to know
The door to my cell is open wide
   and a voice cries out oh no

The judge says I'm guilty my
   sentence is to die
I know I've been forgiven but the
   price of love is high

The crowd outside is screamin' let
   that murderer die
But above all their voices I can hear
   my Mama cry

I'm sittin' here on death row and
   Lord I've lost my mind
For love I've killed my darlin' and
   for love I'll lose my life

I can hear the warden coming from
   the clinging of his keys
But when they come to get me he'll
   have to drag me off my knees
The door to my cell swings open it's
   time for me to go
The priest is reading my last rites
He says dying's part of livin' ya
   know

And there's a crowd outside
   screamin' let that murderer fry
But above all their voices you can
   hear my Mama cry

Now they've strapped me in the
   chair and covered up my eyes
And the last voice I hear on Earth is
   my Mama's cry

Amazing Grace, how sweet the
   sound
That saved a wretch like me
I once was lost, but now am found
Was blind, but now I see

Van Lear Rose Grammy 2005

I tell everybody that the *Van Lear Rose* album was one of the countriest records I ever made. One of the easiest, too. I never dreamed—and I bet Jack didn't, either—when we started making this record that we would end up winning not one but two Grammys! And the record was nominated for more than that.

When Patsy called me and told me we were going to L.A. to go to the Grammys, I said to her, "Why, I ain't gonna win nothin'."

But Patsy is always looking for a reason to buy a new dress, and I'm pretty sure that's really why we went. Jack called me, too, and asked me what I was gonna wear. He had Manuel make him a suit to match my dress!

Well, I have to tell you, I was sitting there at the Grammys with Jack and his manager and Patsy and friends. If you ain't never seen the Grammy show, you're missin' something big! It's all kinds of music, not just country or rock, but *everything*, and it's a big deal, let me tell you! I was a nervous wreck 'cause I would've felt bad for

Jack and Patsy if we didn't win anything. And when I get nervous, I talk and I can't shut up. So I just kept chattering away.

When it was time for the Best Country Record award, they headed our way with the cameras. They wanted to film each artist's face when they announced the nomination. Since I didn't think we would win, I didn't even prepare anything to say. Jack knew I was nervous, so he held my hand. All I remember is seein' little Alison Krauss onstage. I just love her. And when they called my and

Jack's names, I was so shocked I just sat there! I couldn't believe it. And I couldn't move! Patsy started jumping up and down, and Jack stood and helped me up. We walked up there— and friends, that's about all I can remember about the night!

We ended up getting another Grammy for me and Jack singin' "Portland, Oregon," too. I stayed on cloud nine for a whole year! I know Jack did, too. *Van Lear Rose* was a coming-out party for Jack as a producer, and what a party he had!

"Just to Have You Back"

Jack White and I cut twelve songs for the *Van Lear Rose* record project. But we only put eleven on the album. I wished we could have released "Just to Have You Back." It is the song that was left off. One day I'm gonna release this song. I love it so much.

Just to have you back
We were young and crazy in love
Not a dollar in our pocket between
    the two of us
Tired of those coal mine fields we
    left those Kentucky hills
Chasin' fame and fortune with a
    song
If I'd known then what I know now
I'd have put that old guitar down
But I thought we had all the time in
    the world

This king size bed with satin sheets
Meant for two but it's just me
Wasted time keepin' up with the
    Jones

That big old house on the hill we
    called home
But could never fill
Our hearts like that old Kentucky
    shack
I'd give anything give up everything
    just to have you back

I never dreamed that one day you'd
    be gone
And our golden years I would spend
    alone
The kids come by now and then
It brings a smile but then again
Seein' them just makes me miss
    you more

BMI Songwriter

When I first came to Nashville, the Wilburn Brothers took me over to meet Francis Preston at BMI. I am still a BMI writer today. They have always been so good to me, and they've done a great job looking after my songs.

When you're in this business, if you find a place or a person who does a good job for you, stick with 'em. You will have a lot of folks trying to talk you into going with this one or that one. But I am loyal . . . and as long as they do a good job and do right by me, I stay. I don't know how many songs I have through BMI . . . a lot! Heck, I've been singin' and writin' a very long time.

In 2005, BMI honored me in Nashville. It was a very special event for me. They all knew my favorite girl singer and hero was Kitty Wells. So when they brought me in to sit down at this big table, there sit Kitty and Johnny Wright (her husband and singing partner). Kitty and Johnny have been married for over fifty years! That was a thrill for me. My little sister Crystal was there, too. It was so nice for BMI to go to all that trouble to do all that for me. I guess loyalty really does beget loyalty.

2008 Songwriter of the Year

As a songwriter, one of the biggest honors you can get is to be recognized by other songwriters. In 2008 the Songwriters Hall of Fame gave me this honor. The whole thing was in New York City. There were five of us writers getting this honor that night—they had Lee Ann Womack there to sing one of my songs—and I was about the last one. When it came my turn, I thought, I ain't gonna get up there and talk and talk, I'm gonna sing! So I sang "Coal Miner's Daughter."

They had a band there, and they all had learned that song, so it went really good. In fact, I thought it was so good, I decided to sing another. It didn't cross my mind that the band hadn't learned another one of my songs. So, I just sang it without them! Gibson Guitar gave us all the prettiest guitars with the honoree's name printed in pearl on the neck. I put mine over in my museum at my ranch in Hurricane Mills. Looking back over all the awards I've won, I have to say that having these kinds of songs recognized goes to the top of my list of favorites.

"Don't Tempt Me Baby"

WRITTEN WITH Todd D. Snider
RELEASE DATE 2009
ALBUM *The Excitement Plan* (released by
Todd Snider)

Don't tempt me baby
I've got a good thing going at home
Too much to lose
If I don't leave here alone
But don't tempt me baby

You've got my heart locked
Out of your mind
I've found the key
But I have run out of time
I'm trying to walk out of here
Walkin' the line
Don't tempt me baby

In the mirror behind the bar
I could see
That come on over look
That you gave to me
But truly flattering I guarantee
But I'm as spoken for
As you must be free

Don't tempt me baby
I've got a ring around my finger ya
    know
I shoulda headed home a long time
    ago

But don't tempt me baby
I made a promise it was well
    understood
What I couldn't do
And what I could
I'm feelin' weak
And you're lookin' so good
Don't tempt me baby

So now big boy
Don't you flatter yourself
That beer must be showin' you
    somethin' else
You've been sitting here since two
    o'clock
And anyone can see
You're as stoned as a rock

Yeah don't tempt me baby
I've got a good thing going at home
Too much to lose
If I don't leave here alone
Don't tempt me baby

You've got my heart locked
Out of your mind
I've found the key
But I've run out of time
I'm walkin' out of here
Walkin' the line
Don't tempt me baby

"Another Bridge to Burn"

UNRELEASED

I don't suppose I'll ever love him
   quite the way that I love you
But when he slips into my dreams
I don't wake up feeling blue
What we don't have in common
We make up for in concern
I just found another match
You're another bridge it's time to
   burn
Through the years I've cried a river
One tear drop at a time
I kept that old bridge standing
   strong
Just in case you changed your mind
I can't live on dreams forever
At least reality returns
With his hand in mine we'll light
   the flame
You're another bridge it's time to
   burn
Oh I never will forget you
Or a single memory
But he's here now and you're gone
And you make such lonely
   memories
I don't know how to touch him
   right
But I know I want to learn
I just found another match
You're another bridge it's time to
   burn
Through the years I've cried a river
One tear drop at a time
I kept that old bridge standing
   strong

Just in case you changed your mind
I can't live on dreams forever
At least reality returns
With his hand in mine
We'll light the flame
You're another bridge it's time to
   burn

"Better Off Blue"

WRITTEN WITH Patsy Lynn Russell
UNRELEASED

Baby don't you bother knockin'
Stay away from my door
Ain't no use in your sweet talkin'
Sorry don't work no more

I have come to this conclusion
Sense of reality
Boy your love is worth losin'
To save my sanity

Better off blue
I'm better off lonely
I'll learn to live without you
If it's the last thing I do
You're just a pain in my heart
I'll have to work through
It's all black and white
I'm better off blue

You're a bad habit
That needs a breakin'
Gonna take a lot of self-control
Won't be easy but you I'm a shakin'
'Cause baby this much I know

"The Big Man"

WRITTEN WITH Shawn Camp
UNRELEASED

I've been keepin' company
With someone that I love
He's somebody special
Who I can't stop thinkin' of
I want to be right with him
And he tells me I can
When the Big Man's holdin' on to
    my hand

Chorus:
And when I cross over Jordan
Over to that golden shore
I know he'll be waiting there
To love me that much more
No he don't make no footprints
When we walk through the sand
But the Big Man's holdin' on to my
    hand

I talk to him daily
'Cause we always stay in touch
He's right there when I need him
Oh I need him oh so much
I'd love to be more faithful
And devoted than I am
'Cause the Big Man's holdin' on to
    my hand

And when I cross over Jordan
Over to that golden shore
I know he'll be waiting there
To love me that much more
He don't make no footprints
When we walk through the sand
But the Big Man's holdin' on to my
    hand

No he don't make no footprints
When we walk through the sand
But the Big Man's holdin' on to my
    hand

"Blue Blue Heartaches"

WRITTEN WITH The Lynns
UNRELEASED

When I walked away and said we're
    through
Never counted on the part about
    these blues
Now what am I gonna say and do
I want you back
But I know you will refuse

Blue Blue Heartaches
Blue Blue Heartaches
Every time I think I'm over you
Blue Blue Heartaches

You told me when I left just what
    I'd lose
I turned my back on the love
That we once knew
When I see you out with someone
    new
Every tear that falls comes from a
    fool

Blue Blue Heartaches
Blue Blue Heartaches
Every time I think I'm over you
Blue Blue Heartaches

Onstage, 2008

"Bluer Than Ever"

WRITTEN WITH The Lynns
UNRELEASED

They say the tears will stop in time
But mine ain't
And I'll forget about you baby
But I can't
Each day it seems to hurt
Just a little bit more
It's gettin' worse not better
I'm bluer than ever

I'm bluer than ever
I can't get past this pain
It feels like forever
Never gonna go away
Each morning till night
24/7 all the time
It never gets better
I'm bluer than ever

My friends tell me a night on the
   town
A good time
A stranger to talk to
Over a glass of wine
But I can't pick myself up
Much less out the door
I'm in for bad weather
I'm bluer than ever

"Break Free"

WRITTEN WITH Patsy Lynn Russell
UNRELEASED

That man brought her nothing but
   a heartache
And she fatefully wears the pain
She's tried hanging on
Through thick and thin
As he breaks every promise he's
   made
She can't find the strength to leave
   him
Convinced herself she's part to
   blame
So she'll go through what only she
   can undo
Until she breaks free from the chain

Break free from the chain
Around her heart
She sees no way out

But last night he came home full of
   whiskey
Started getting loud and mean
But this time he pushed her one
   time too often
So she waited until he was asleep

Packed only what she could carry
Made a bed for the kids in the car
She had no idea where she was
    going

"Broad-Minded Man"

WRITTEN WITH Jay Lee Webb
UNRELEASED

I'm a broad-minded man, that's
    what my woman tells me.
She can't see the reason why, girls
    are all I see.
Says I better start to straighten
    up real quick, but I can't change
    what I am
'Cause I got women on my brain,
    I'm a broad-minded man.

I got a one-track mind, there's no
    two ways about it.
I'm not ashamed that I like girls,
    and I don't try to hide it.

My little woman, she comes from
    the hills,
But I like bottomland, and she don't
    like my raisin' Cain,
But I'm a broad-minded man.

I'm a broad-minded man, I'm as
    happy as I can be
I'll keep on a lookin' at girls as long
    as I can see
The little woman says that I'm a
    gonna go blind,
But she don't understand, with
    both eyes open or closed,
I'm a broad-minded man.

I got a one-track mind, there's no
    two ways about it.
I'm not ashamed that I like girls,
    and I don't try to hide it.
My little woman, she comes from
    the hills,
But I like bottomland, and she don't
    like my raisin' Cain,
But I'm a broad-minded man.

Loretta with Muhammad
Ali, 1990

"Copper Basin Mother of the Year"

WRITTEN WITH Lorene Allen
UNRELEASED

Down in Copper Basin, that's where
　Peggy Allen waits
For a jury to decide what will be her
　fate
The mother of five children, the
　youngest Lora Mae
Peggy shot their father and may
　have to go away

Victim of a dread disease, little Lora
　Mae has suffered
And wouldn't be alive today if it
　wasn't for her mother

Each week they go to Memphis and
　the trips keep her alive
That's where she takes her
　treatments, this little girl of five

The children range in age from five
　years to fifteen
Gail and Bobby, Aronoff, Lora Mae
　and Marleen
They often begged their mother to
　take them and go away
She's explained their dad was sick
　and that they'd have to stay

Back in early August, was on the
　seventh day
Peggy'd been to Memphis, she and
　little Lora Mae

Came home and found her husband
   very drunk and very mean
He had thrown a knife at Gail and
   almost killed Marleen.

That awful Wednesday evening
   Peggy took her husband's life
To protect her children, mother
   overshadowed wife
Robert Allen laughed and bragged
   that he'd kill them everyone
Peggy had to make a choice and it
   was not an easy one

Robert Allen was a man sick in body
   and in mind
And people who know Peggy know
   she's not the killing kind
Even if she's parted from the ones
   she holds so dear
The folks in Copper Basin named
   her mother of the year

"Cold Christmas"

WRITTEN WITH Philip Russell
UNRELEASED

Chorus:
Gonna be a cold, cold Christmas
Think I'll decorate my tree in blue
Gonna be a cold, cold Christmas
Without you to snuggle up to

'Tis the season to be jolly
With all the holiday cheer
But the forecast is calling for lonely
Gonna be a cold Christmas this year

This record-breaking low
Has really got me down
That time of year again
When the snow covers the ground
And old Jack Frost
Will chill me to the bone
'Cause this cold Christmas
I will spend alone

Chorus:
Gonna be a cold, cold Christmas
Think I'll decorate my tree in blue
Gonna be a cold, cold Christmas
Without you to snuggle up to
'Tis the season to be jolly
With all the holiday cheer
But the forecast is calling for lonely
Gonna be a cold Christmas this year

Think I'll build myself a fire
Like we used to do
Reminisce with the mem'ries
To help me make it through
That's all that's left
Since all hope for us is gone
Unless a miracle happens
And ol' Santa brings you home

[Repeat chorus]

"The Door"

UNRELEASED

I'm tired of you wiping your feet
across my heart
Like it was an old doormat
You've stepped on me so many
times
You don't even realize, you've
smashed my love for you flat
Well I'm picking myself up, babe
I've had enough
Ain't gonna be your walking path
no more
Gonna be the door

The door you'll hear slamming
Pictures you'll see landing
Broken to pieces on the floor
The note you'll be reading
Giving all the reasons
Why I ain't coming back no more
The footsteps you'll hear walking
The car you'll hear starting
And the bang that's come right
before
Me slamming the door

You'll wonder what happened to
that innocent girl you once knew
That sure you could do no wrong
Well she finally smarted up, took
your misbehaving long enough
Learned to do some walking of her
own
So sorry to tell you this but maybe
you'll get my jest at the door
I ain't taking it no more

"Down Among the Wine and Spirits"

WRITTEN WITH Elvis Costello
UNRELEASED

Down among the wine and spirits
Where a man gets what he
merits . . .
Once it was written nine feet tall
Now he sees how far he has fallen

Since he set his mind on her
completely
Then I guess that you couldn't have
seen him lately
Walking around with a pain that
never ceases
He starts to speak and then he goes
to pieces . . .

Down among the wine and spirits
Where a man gets what he
merits . . .
Lives with the echo words of their
final quarrel
The vacant chamber
The empty barrel

As he picks his self up from a
sawdust floor
Clicks his fingers to the swinging
door
Suddenly he's calling out, "More,
more, more . . .
Down among the wine and spirits

Bubbles escaping from him from
the rim a glass of grape
She sails through his memory just
like a ship of shapely
He started to sink he was drinking
to drown his sorrows

That fill his nights and empty
   tomorrows

As he picks his self up from the
   sawdust floor
Clicks his fingers to the swinging
   door
Suddenly he's calling out, "More,
   more, more . . ."

Down among the wine and spirits
Down among the wine and spirits
Down among the wine and spirits
Down among the wine and spirits
Down among the wine and spirits

"Every Door You Opened"

UNRELEASED

You left me alone too many nights
When you had no excuse
But the one you made up in your
   mind
Your wedding band was too loose
I know the hurt you're hurting now
Is like the hurt that you gave me
And every door you opened up
You opened up for me

Love is like a fruit that you grow on
   trees
If you don't pick the fruit
The tree will die you see
That's what happened to our love
Yes you neglected me
Every door you opened up
You opened up for me

The way I act and the way I look
Ain't the way I want to be
But you left me no choice but to
   end this misery
So don't tell me I done you wrong
And cry for sympathy
'Cause every door you opened up
You opened up for me

"Falling Again"

UNRELEASED

Well here you come again
And I start talking to my heart
You're crazy he's taken
Please don't let him win
But when you take my hand and say
Please try to understand
I stumble and fall
And fall all over myself again

Yeah here we are the two of us
On the outside looking in
Wanting to be lovers
Trying hard to be friends
I'm reaching for a rainbow
And chasing the wind
Doggone this heart
It's falling all over again

Lord I feel I'm giving in
I think I'm going to let you win
There's something inside of me
That pulls me right back into your
   arms again
You wouldn't be here if you were
   happy
You say where and I'll say when
Lord here I go falling all over again

We got 2 Hundred pictures
Made of that picture of mine
for Pomotion to day.

4 - 20 - 60

My Dearest Darling
It ofaut 7 oclock in the Euening
and I'm rull tired. We just got fock from
Hollywood. it ofaut 70 Miles from here.
Well Honey here I am fock ogain I had
to Stof wrighting to go have Supper. I Had
another stoke for dinner I had a griled
Ham & Cheese with a piece of pie and milk
this Morning I had Eggs potatoes and bacon
with Orange Juice. Darling I miss you so
Much you are all I thonk of. Honey We Went
to one D J to day he Was rull glad to
have Me come he interuud me and ployed
both Sides of my record While I Was
thier I told him I Would Send him
a Picture as Soon as I got fock home
he Said I had a buotiful Voice
he Said he would ploy the threds

"Every Time We Go to Bed"

WRITTEN WITH The Lynns
UNRELEASED

Trouble always starts under the
   covers
And lately there's been trouble here
   with me
I think that you have found your
   self another
'Cause every time we go to bed you
   go to sleep

There's no hugging and no kissin'
No more tangled sheets
The bed that used to rock
Now don't make a peep
When we turn out the lights
It's back to back not cheek to cheek
Every time we go to bed you go to
   sleep

I've had this strange suspicion for
   some time
A woman's intuition you call a
   jealous mind
But when the lights go out
It's back to back not cheek to cheek
Every time we go to bed you go to
   sleep

There's no hugging and no kissin'
No more tangled sheets
The bed that used to rock
Now don't make a peep
When we turn out the lights
It's back to back not cheek to cheek
Every time we go to bed you go to
   sleep

"Feel the Love"

WRITTEN WITH Philip Russell
UNRELEASED

Oh do you
Feel the love
Feel the love
All around you
Oh do you
Feel the love
Feel the love
All around you

Oh my dear
It's not really all that bad
We got the sunshine
And another day
Take my hand
Look in my eyes
Hold me close
Tell me what do you find

Oh do you
Feel the love
Feel the love
Feel the love
I have for you
Oh do you
Feel the love
Feel the love
Love in your heart

"For a Boy Who Has Nothing"

UNRELEASED

Well you say that you've got
   nothing
Nothing to offer but a poor boy's
   love
But with you I have everything
I could ever want
For a boy who has nothing
You sure do something to me

For a boy who has nothing
You sure do something to me
Your love I'd never trade
For all the treasures in the sea
I'm the luckiest girl I know
With you is where I want to be
For a boy who has nothing
You sure do something to me

Diamonds you can't buy me
No mansion to call home
To me those things mean nothing
You can't buy the love
You give your giving so free
For a boy who has nothing
You sure do something to me

"For the Life of Me"

UNRELEASED

For the life of me, I can't see what
   you see in her,
But you seem to be satisfied by her
   side, no matter where.
What does she do that I don't do,
   will you teach me what she does
   for you?
If you will, I'll prove I'm still twice
   the woman that she is.

For the life of me, I can't see what
   you see in her.
I love you, that's all I know.
Please don't go to her and leave me
   standing here.
If you'll give me a little time, I'm
   gonna love her right off your
   mind.
But for the life of me, I can't see
   what you see in her.

"Gonna Live and Die on This Ole Farm"

UNRELEASED

Well this old farmhouse has gone
  to the dogs
It used to be purty till I let out the
  hogs, they rooted up ten acres of
  land
And I'm getting ready to have me
  some ham
Yea this old farmer's gone to, well
  I'll fix the fences but it wouldn't
  sell
I ain't got nothing to be happy
  about
Yep my baby ran off when the
  money ran out

Well this old farm to me is Heaven
I've been blessed I got kids eleven
I may wander, but I don't get far
I'm gonna live and die on this old
  farm

I'm gonna live and die on this old
  farm

Well this old farm may fall to the
  ground
It don't matter nobody comes
  around
That old rooster ain't crowed in
  days
He says he ain't gonna crow till that
  chicken lays

Yea this old farm to me is Heaven
I've been blessed I got kids eleven
I may wander, but I don't get far
I'm gonna live and die on this old
  farm
I'm gonna live and die on this old
  farm

Well this old farm to me is Heaven
I've been blessed I got kids eleven
I may wander, but I don't get far
I'm gonna live and die on this old
  farm

Loretta at home, 1980s

163

I'm gonna live and die on this old
farm

I'm gonna live and die on this old
farm
I'm gonna live and die on this old
farm
I'm gonna live and die on this old
farm

I'm gonna live and die on this old
farm

"Forever Yours"

WRITTEN WITH Philip Russell and Patsy
Lynn Russell
UNRELEASED

Loretta with Barbara
Walters, 1982

Deep as the ocean floor
Long as the rivers flow
I'll be forever yours
Sure as the sun will rise

Way past the end of time
I'll be forever yours

We were meant to be
Always eternally
Nothing can keep us apart
Our love won't fade away
It's for keeps come what may
I'll be forever yours

We were meant to be
Always eternally
Nothing can keep us apart
Our love won't fade away
It's for keeps come what may
I'll be . . . forever yours
I'll be . . . forever yours
Forever yours . . .

"Gotta Love That"

WRITTEN WITH Philip Russell
UNRELEASED

The bills are paid the weekend's
  here
A clear blue sky and an ice cold beer
My fishin' pole and my lucky ol' cap
Oh you gotta love that

And my wife says, "Mom will keep
  the kids all day"
A little time alone so we can play—
Lock the door and jump in that sack
  (ha, ha)
Ooh, gotta love that

Chorus:
Yeah gotta love that—
Ain't no mistake about it
 Ya love that—
And there ain't no way around it
Oh everything's good and going my
  way
Ain't no rain gonna ruin my parade
Sun is shining right here on my lap
And you gotta love that
Yeah gotta love that

"Grass May Be Greener"

UNRELEASED

Well you're grazing in a pasture
Where you know you don't belong
Yeah the only thing that's growing
  there
Is the wild seeds that's been sowed
Just move on out and move in this
This one thing you should know
That grass may be greener
But it's just as hard to mow

Well take everything you can haul
You'll need everything you got
'Cause as fast as her grass grows
You're gonna have to mow a lot
Even in the winter it still seems to
  grow
Yeah the grass may be greener
But it's just as hard to mow

Well it seems like you can't write
To all this
That's what happens to a man
When a woman's on his mind
Go on and get it,
I guess you think that I don't know
Yeah grass may be greener
But it's just as hard to mow

Loretta with Gregory Peck,
1981

"Half a Woman"

UNRELEASED

Lord I've got something on my
   mind
And it's driving me insane
I can't tell the man I love
I am too ashamed
This sin I've done,
Lord I know it would break most
   any man
'Cause I'm only half
Half the woman he thinks I am

Yes I'm only half the woman
Half the woman he thinks I am

I sent my pride to find my
   conscience
With my tarnished wedding band
So when I die just bury me only
   three feet down
'Cause I'm only half the woman
I don't deserve six feet of ground

I can't look him in the eye
I'm too scared that he may see
The one he holds so precious
Is no longer so worthy
With my guilt I'll go on living
And do the best I can
'Cause I'm only half the woman
Half the woman he thinks I am

"He Wasn't Talking to Me"

WRITTEN WITH Patsy Lynn Russell
UNRELEASED

Tenderly he whispered I love you
From the shadows in a voice so
  sincere
I felt the tears start
When he said forever sweetheart
'Cause he wasn't talking to me

I hung on every word he was sayin'
As he poured out his heart in a
  secret conversation
He said everything that I long to
  hear so clear
But he wasn't talking to me

I just stood there and listened for a
  moment
My heart breaking from what I just
  heard
I couldn't not believe as I fell to my
  knees
He wasn't talking to me

"Have You Ever Wronged"

UNRELEASED

Have you ever wronged the one
  you love
And you don't know the reason
  why

When the one you love
Means more to you
Than all the stars in the sky

Each night I sit and wonder why
What a foolish thing I've done
I betrayed I strayed to another's
  arm
And wronged the one I love

Have you ever wronged the one
  you love
And you don't know the reason
  why
When the one you wrong
Means more to you
Than all the stars in the sky

I told my love I'm sorry but
He say he can't forgive
I watched him leave begged him
  please
Now in shame I'll have to live

Have you ever wronged the one
  you love
And you don't know the reason
  why
When the one you love
Means more to you
Than all the stars in the sky

Have you ever wronged the one
  you love

"Hurting All Over Again"

UNRELEASED

Well when my baby left I tried to
  go on
But the hurting just kept hurting
From midnight 'til dawn
I told my mind to forget you
But my heart keeps nosing in
And I'm hurting all over again

Hurting all over again
A heartache that just won't end
I try and I try but my tears never
  dry
And I'm hurting all over again

Everyone keeps telling me it takes
  time
I have to move on with my life
In this misery, I'm paralyzed
It won't let me sleep, won't let me
  rise
Oh I'm hurting all over again

"I Never Stopped Lovin' You"

WRITTEN WITH The Lynns
UNRELEASED

I should've known but my feelings
  felt a little low
So I pack up my things in search for
  something more
I was running from you this love
Heading out the door
I was looking for adventure
Didn't know what lied in store
Oh baby I never stopped lovin' you

I never stopped lovin' you
Not even for a second or two
I'm sorry baby I've been such a fool
What can I do to make this up to
  you
I swear baby it's true
I never stopped lovin' you

I was lookin' for something headin'
  down that lonesome road
But deep inside my heart I could
  never let you go
Now I won't pretend to you I don't
  feel the things I do
You can walk away from me God
  knows I walked away from you

[Repeat chorus]

"I Can See Through You"

WRITTEN WITH The Lynns
UNRELEASED

The first time I saw him he took me
  by surprise
Felt this wave of emotion haven't
  felt in some time
The feel of him still took my breath
But the change in him says we've
  never met

Chorus:
But don't you know
I can see through you
I can see through you
So you go and be who you need
And believe what you want to
  believe
I can see through you
See through you

A stranger in my eyes that's all he
  was
The only thing familiar was a
  glance given up
I wanted to reach out take him
  from this change
But I knew in my heart it would
  never be the same

Chorus:
But don't you know
I can see through you
I can see through you
So you go and be who you need
And believe what you want to
  believe
I can see through you
See through you

"I'm Dyin' for Someone to Live For"

WRITTEN WITH Shawn Camp
UNRELEASED

Loneliness falls all around
And it's almost got me down
Well I guess when it rains it pours
I'm dyin' for someone to live for
There's a whip-poor-will out on a
  limb
Yeah I know I'm more lonesome
  than him
Now I don't know what he's cryin'
  for

I'm dyin' for someone to live for
And the weepin' willow cries
Every time a good love says
  goodbye
I hear the tide comin' in on the
  shore
I'm dyin' for someone to live for

The love of my life is long gone
And I don't know what I've done so
  wrong
I don't think I can take too much
  more
I'm dyin' for someone to live for

And the weepin' willow cries
Every time a good love says
  goodbye
I hear the tide comin' in on the
  shore
I'm dyin' for someone to live for

Lord, I'm dyin' for someone to live
  for

Loretta is original—
she is enduring, sexy, and
always . . . cool.

GARTH BROOKS

"I'm on the Loose"

UNRELEASED

I'm hangin' on with everything I got
Everything I got is almost shot
That's O.K. Mr. Gander
You've already cooked your goose
I'm breaking this chain, here's your
    ring
Your baby's on the loose

Yeah, I'm turning loose
I'm gonna rock and swing
Like I've never swang before
'Cause baby there ain't no use
I'm breaking this chain
I hate this thing
Your baby's on the loose

I'm turning loose, Lord I feel free
You can watch me fly away
I got tired of hanging on
So I lost my mind today
I've had doubt while you're
    making up
Another bad excuse
I broke the chain, I'm gonna sling
    this thing
Yeah your baby's on the loose

"I'm Gonna Make Like a Snake"

UNRELEASED

I get off from work every day at
    five,
And by five of five you'll find me in
    this dive.

When I'm a sober man, I stand real
    tall.
When I'm a drinking man, I have to
    crawl.
I'm gonna make like a snake and
    crawl right outa here.

I'm gonna make like a snake and
    crawl right outa here,
I couldn't hold my baby any
    better'n I could hold my beer.
When my mind gets drunk I don't
    seem to care if I never so lay eyes
    on her,
I'm gonna make like a snake and
    crawl right outa here.

When my baby said, "I'm leavin'
    you big man!"
That's when my drinking got all out
    of hand.
So pour me one more glass of
    cheer, pay no mind to these
    drunks 'n' tears,
I'm gonna make like a snake and
    crawl right outa here.

I'm gonna make like a snake and
    crawl right outa here,
I couldn't hold my baby any
    better'n I could hold my beer.
When my mind gets drunk I don't
    seem to care if I never so lay eyes
    on her,
I'm gonna make like a snake and
    crawl right outa here.

OPPOSITE Loretta with
Garth Brooks

"I'm Bound to Lose Control"

UNRELEASED

Please don't try to tempt me any
 longer
'Cause my pride is getting weaker
 and my passion's getting
 stronger.
Tell me you don't want me, and
 turn around and go.
If you try to love me, I'm bound to
 lose control.

I'm bound to lose control, and I'll
 lose everything I own.
Then I won't wake up till
 everything I have is gone.
If you lay your hand on me, you'll
 feel I'm warm, not cold.
If you try to love me, I'm bound to
 lose control.

You're everything I want, so I keep
 tryin'
To keep from givin' in to you but
 my will is slowly dyin'.
My conscience says too late for me
 and I don't do what I'm told.
If you try to love me, I'm bound to
 lose control.

I'm bound to lose control, and I'll
 lose everything I own.
Then I won't wake up till
 everything I have is gone.
If you lay your hand on me, you'll
 feel I'm warm, not cold.
If you try to love me, I'm bound to
 lose control.

"If You Don't Want My Love"

WRITTEN WITH The Lynns
UNRELEASED

I can't keep clinging to you when
 you push me away baby
And I can't keep talking to you if
 you don't hear a word I say
All my cards are on the table
Oh and I can feel you pull away
And I can't keep bluffing you when
 you know I have no ace

If you don't want my love, I don't
 need this
If you don't want my touch, I don't
 need this
And I can't go on trying to find a
 way to get to you
If you don't want my love, I don't
 need this

I've been running in circles trying to
 find a way baby
Out of this stagnant stage we seem
 to be going through
My heart is on the line here
Oh and I can't stop this quest to
 find
The answers that I need to feel
 secure with you

"It's You"

WRITTEN WITH Patsy Lynn Russell
UNRELEASED

Well call me crazy
I know how this must sound
But when I saw you baby
There was no doubt
And when we kissed
Baby I knew
The one I had been waiting on
It's you

It's you oh baby yes it's fate
It's you
My heart's so sure yes it's true
It's you

Perfect strangers
Brought together by chance no
Destiny honey I think so
It's written in the stars
Yes it's true
It's you

Walk of Fame, 1980s

"Journey to the End of My World"

WRITTEN WITH Hank Beach
UNRELEASED

Day by day I grew farther away
　　from your love,
My deceitful cheating ways have
　　given me a shove.
Heading straight for destruction,
　　I'm a crazy mixed-up girl.
On a journey to the end of my
　　world.

Oh, if I could only turn back the
　　pages of time,
And rekindle the sweet love that
　　was once yours and mine.
But it's just wishful thinking from
　　this crazy, mixed-up girl.
On a journey to the end of my
　　world.

The end of my world is comin' in
　　view,
And the hurt is so painful, but
　　there's nothing I can do.
I can't shake this low-down feelin'
　　that's come over this girl,
On a journey to the end of my
　　world.

"Lonely Is Not the Only Game in Town"

WRITTEN WITH Philip Russell
UNRELEASED

She waited there 'til nine
Called her mom and said she'd pick
　　the kids up Sunday
She's really leavin' him this time
Make a new start with what little
　　she put away
Lonely is not the only game in town

Bought herself a sexy dress
Had all day to get ready for the
　　night
She wants to look her best
Black stilettos with her hair down
Lonely is not the only game in town

We only get one life
She's gotta have more
Her lucky streak is waiting
Right outside the door

In the morning light she wakes
In a big place with nice marble
　　floors
And a note that just says thanks
She remembers what she's there
　　for
Lonely is not the only game in town
Oh lonely is not the only game in
　　town

OPPOSITE Loretta with
John Travolta, 1982

"Lonely Loretta"

WRITTEN WITH Philip Russell
UNRELEASED

And he left her
Sometime ago
Left for that castle
Up in the sky
Yeah she misses him
But she don't let it show
'Cept when she's all alone
And hangs her head to cry

Chorus:
Lonely Loretta
Sings her sad country song
Lonely Loretta
Don't stay lonely too long

Oh she's got the road
To keep her busy
It helps keep the hurt
From sinkin' in
Yeah and it works
But only for the moment
'Til that last curtain falls
And ol' lonely walks in . . . singin'

[Repeat chorus]

"Lee Dollar Hyde"

UNRELEASED

I'm gonna tell you a story
Of a man named Lee Dollar Hyde
From Kentucky on the Appalachian
    side
Had a moonshine still tucked deep
    into the ridge
And all the town folk knew runnin'
    moonshine was what he did

In those parts there was two things
    a man could do
And Lee was known for his smooth
    mountain brew
The dark coal mine was deep and
    took many lives
And not a resting place for a man
    like Lee Dollar Hyde
Not a resting place for a man like
    Lee Dollar Hyde

Well the revenuer man knew Lee
    was up to no good
But Lee was sly like moonshine
    Robin Hood
And revenuer man couldn't win and
    wanted Lee to pay
Pay for the shine and the jokes the
    town folk made
He'd pay for the shine and jokes the
    town folk made

I'll never forget that cold winter
    day
Cold day revenuer's gun took Lee
    away
When they laid him in the ground
    the sky cried

Or was it only tears on my face for
    Lee Dollar Hyde
Only tears on my face for Lee Dollar
    Hyde

"Loved You All I Can"

UNRELEASED

You look so disappointed with the
    words I've got to say
But you know they're true
And you ask yourself how could she
    just walk away from love
But haven't you

Oh I've loved you all I can
But I can't go on pretending we're
    not through
Oh I've loved you all I can
And somewhere deep inside I guess
    I still do
I've loved you all I can

Too many sleepless nights I guess
Have disillusioned my head and
    clouded up my eyes
And these tears that's falling down
    now are only there to recognize
It's time to say goodbye

Look inside your heart you'll know
    it's true
Somewhere deep inside yourself
    you'll feel it too
I've loved you all I can

"Miner's Widow"

UNRELEASED

She was as pretty as a wild
    mountain flower
He, handsome young and strong
They vowed to each other to love
    one another
For forever and beyond

She walks the fields calling his
    name out
Searching for the body they never
    found
Hear her weeping, when the full
    moon is out
She's the miner's widow

A year was all they shared, he died
    in that coal mine
Her grief never faded away
Her broken heart killed her,
Her ghost haunts this ol' mine
Where she waits for her lover to
    return

She walks the field calling his name
    out
Searching for the body they never
    found
Hear her weeping, when the full
    moon is out
She's the miner's widow

Loretta with John Wayne

"New Orleans"

UNRELEASED

Well I was waiting tables
At a truck stop outside of New
　Orleans
I looked up and come walking in
The best-looking thing I think I've
　ever seen
He said coffee and a doughnut I see
　you just opened up
And girl if you have time I'll even
　buy you a cup

Lord there's no place on earth like
　New Orleans

You never know how much this
　place means to me
If you don't believe me, come down
　and you will see
A little piece of heaven, down here
　in New Orleans

Now there's footprints in the
　hallway
Little handprints on the walls
Laughter fills the rafters
Every day's like Mardi Gras
All these years together whoever
　would believe
A cup of coffee brought us together
Here in New Orleans

"More Alone When I'm with You"

WRITTEN WITH Shawn Camp
UNRELEASED

You don't say two words to me
 when I come in
And you don't even care enough
To ask me where I've been
I swear sometimes you make me
 feel
Like I'm not even home
I'm more alone when I'm with you
Than I am when I'm alone

Chorus:
When I'm alone I'm lonesome oh,
But I don't feel as blue
As I do when you're around
To break my heart in two
Wish I could find a love someplace
Where I felt I belonged
'Cause I'm more alone when I'm
 with you
Than I am when I'm alone

When we go out and we walk side
 by side
I wonder if our friends can tell
Our love is not alive
From the outside it might look a lot
 like
There ain't nothin' wrong
But I'm more alone when I'm with
 you
Than I am when I'm alone

Chorus:
When I'm alone I'm lonesome oh,
But I don't feel as blue
As I do when you're around

To break my heart in two
Wish I could find a love someplace
Where I felt I belonged
'Cause I'm more alone when I'm
 with you
Than I am when I'm alone

"Night to Forget"

WRITTEN WITH Philip Russell
UNRELEASED

Drank a little too much last night
And made an (ass, fool) of myself
Crying over what might have been
If she hadn't found that someone
 else
Yeah I guess it's embarrassing
Oh but I don't really care
But if I could do it over again
I'd rather not have fell down the
 stairs—

Chorus:
Yeah that would be . . . a
 night . . . to forget
One day in my life that I wished I'd
 never met
I liked to lose that memory oh but I
 still haven't yet—
I keep on remem'ring that night to
 forget

Said she needed some time alone
Things were moving a little too fast
I knew she needed her space to
 breathe
If it was ever gonna last
So I went out to drink a beer
And give myself some space too

Then she comes walking in
Holding hands with someone new

Chorus:
Yeah that would be . . . a night to
    forget
One day in my life that I wish I'd
    never met
I like to lose that memory oh but I
    haven't yet—
I keep on remem'ring that night to
    forget

"On My Way to Nashville"

WRITTEN WITH James Lipton
UNRELEASED

There's a great big world
Stretchin' far and wide
Callin' me to my magic carpet ride
So I've packed my hopes and
    favorite schemes
And I'm on my way to my land of
    dreams

On my way
Hey hey
I'm on my way to Nashville
On my way
Hey hey
I'm on my way to Nashville,
    Tennessee

Well I got my song
And my big guitar
Before too long
I'll be an Opry star

Gonna beat that drum
Gonna ring them bells
Just like Patsy Cline
Just like Kitty Wells

'Cause I'm on my way
Hey hey
I'm on my way to Nashville
On my way
Hey hey
On my way to Nashville, Tennessee

Come fly with me
Come fly
Come fly away

I'd said we'd make Nashville or bust
Look down Nashville
Lookin' up at us

Hey Grand Ole Opry
Open wide make room
For one more star inside
Yeah, stand back Ernest, Glenn, and
    Roy
Here comes a brand-new country
    boy

Look out Tammy and Minnie Pearl
Here comes another country girl

We're on our way
Hey hey
We're on our way to Nashville
Here today
Hey hey
We're here to stay in Nashville,
    Tennessee

Loretta with Faith Hill, 1993

Loretta with John
Mellencamp, 1985

"Patchwork Quilt"

WRITTEN WITH Lorene Allen
UNRELEASED

It's just a patchwork quilt—that's
    all it is
But to me, it means a whole lot
    more than this
It's a patchwork story, told by my
    mama's hands
Now let me tell you of the things
    for which the patches stand

There's a scrap from a shirt Mom
    made for Dad
He said it was the nicest shirt he'd
    ever had
Tiny prints for baby sis—we loved
    her so
Oh but she took sick and died when
    she was two years old

First Chorus:
Striped flannel from pajamas with
    the feet built in
How I wish I could live those old
    days again
But as close to yesterday as I'll ever
    get
Is Mama's patchwork quilt—
    because it's all that's left

That blue velvet—it's from my first
    evening dress
Some bright red wool left over
    from big brother's vest
Both of us so proud and dressed-up
    fit to kill
Pages from the past in Mama's
    patchwork quilt

It almost killed Mama when we
    buried Dad

But she went right on sewing while
    her eyes went bad
She made herself a lovely dress of
    orchid silk
And put some pieces of it in her
    patchwork quilt

Second Chorus:
She finished up the quilt and then
    she sewed no more
The orchid dress she'd saved for
    good she finally wore
I look at all the remnants and I
    reminisce
My mama was an angel in her
    orchid dress

"Rescue Me"

UNRELEASED

Somebody rescue me
This man's got his hands all over me
Don't stand there and act like you
    can't see
Oh won't somebody rescue me

This man winked at me a time or
    two
He grabbed my arm and said I want
    to dance with you
But I'm a married woman, you
    better let me be
Oh won't somebody rescue me

Well there's a big ol' blanket on the
    ground
Won't somebody catch me
'Cause I think I'm going down
Play like a good New Yorker

And act like you can't see
No don't nobody try to rescue me

What he don't know won't hurt
    him I tell myself
If he finds out what I'm doing it'll
    be from someone else
But right now I'm loving this
    stranger loving me
Oh won't somebody rescue me

"No Lady's Man"

UNRELEASED

Well you know my heart is way too
    soft
I love you way too hard
But it's my mistake for what I take
But I'm finally getting tired
Tired of the way you treat me
But on the other hand
Just want you to know
I'm smart enough to know that
    you're
A lady's man

A lady's man is what you are
And have been all the time
I'm not as dumb as you think
And I think you think I'm blind
You go looking for something
    different
Ain't that just like a man
Just want you to know
I'm smart enough to know
That you're a lady's man

You tell me that you love me
And I really think you do

So you know what, I'm going
    looking
For someone better to latch on to
'Cause you ain't going honey
And I don't believe you can
But just letting you know
I'm smart enough to know
That you're a lady's man

"Ruby's Stool"

WRITTEN WITH Shawn Camp
UNRELEASED

She's been dancin' all night with my
    man
Thought about cuttin' in oh but I
    can't
'Cause I'm gonna sit right here
And empty her ashtray into her
    beer
I can't wait to see her drinkin' from
    that can
I'm sittin' on Ruby's stool
Right next to Bill
She likes breakin' ole Bill's heart
And she always will
A honky tonk girl oughta know
    better
Than to break the rules
I'm fed up with her
So I'm sittin' on Ruby's stool
Everybody always gives her lots of
    space
No one would ever dare get in her
    face
I ain't never been one to fight
But friends tonight's the night

And I'm just the gal to put her in
    her place
I'm sittin' on Ruby's stool
Right next to Bill
She likes breakin' ole Bill's heart
And she always will
A honky tonk girl oughta know
    better
Than to break the rules
I'm fed up with her
So I'm sittin' on Ruby's stool

"Sittin' Bull"

WRITTEN WITH Lorene Allen
UNRELEASED

Now, listen to ol' Sittin' Bull, I just
    about got my craw full,
There's talk on reservation, and
    there's even talk in town.
They say my squaw and white man
    play,
That you like the white man's way
    and ol' Sittin' Bull
Ain't gonna take it sittin' down.

Ol' Sittin' Bull ain't a gonna take it
    sittin' down,
Ain't no white man gonna stomp
    my stompin' ground.
You can call him your blood brother,
    don't carry this carryin' on no
    further,

'Cause Sittin' Bull ain't gonna take
    it sittin' down.

"Playin' After Dark"

UNRELEASED

You've got a habit that I can't
    break, a playin' after dark,
I finally found your playground but
    you use it for a park.
So go on out and play, but don't
    worry about the time,
'Cause your sweet mama's got a
    few little things in mind.

You do your playin' after dark and I
    think you're playin' dirty.
Don't ask me who told me this.
    Let's just say a little birdie.
Well, you say you're a playin' a
    game of fun that's as old as
    Noah's ark,

But your fun game's getting a little
    strange after dark.

You've been a playin' every night,
    but tomorrow's Mother's Day.
When you leave to go to work, your
    baby's gonna play.
Well any game your playmates
    play, I know one that's better
Your mama found her a tall, dark
    babysitter.

You do your playin' after dark and I
    think you're playin' dirty.
Don't ask me who told me this.
    Let's just say a little birdie.
Well, any game your playmates
    play, I know one that's better,
Your fun game's getting a little
    strange after dark.

Loretta with Kenny Rogers

185

"She Can't Forget"

WRITTEN WITH The Lynns
UNRELEASED

She sleeps all alone in a bed meant
for couples
Holdin' a picture of him in her
hands
What once was a fire has now
turned to ashes
And she can't forget to stop
remembering him

She knows that it's over, she knows
that they're through
Hangin' on to a memory that she
can't hold loose
She recalls every detail right down
to the end
But she can't forget to stop
remembering him

She cries out in the darkness why
have I been forsaken
A constant reminder she ain't near
the end

The only sound is her own heart
breakin'
But she can't forget to stop
remembering him

She knows that it's over, she knows
that they're through
Hangin' on to a memory that she
can't hold loose
She recalls every detail right down
to the end
But she can't forget to stop
remembering him

She cries out in the darkness why
have I been forsaken
A constant reminder she ain't near
the end
The only sound is her own heart
breakin'
But she can't forget to stop
remembering him
Carryin' on no further.

OPPOSITE Loretta with
Lionel Richie

187

"She's Got Everything It Takes"

WRITTEN WITH Todd Snider
UNRELEASED

I love you more than she ever will
But the only way she can get a man
  is to steal
I don't know if I should tell you this
  or not
She's got everything it takes to take
  everything you've got
And when she takes you
She's taken everything that I've got
  too
She's had a million old flames
So to her you're nothin' new
She's cold as ice but you still think
  she's hot
She's got everything it takes to take
  everything you've got
She turned you on then you turned
  on me
I'm more of a woman than she will
  ever be
To me she ain't nothin' but to her
  that's a lot
She's got everything it takes to take
  everything you've got
And when she takes you she's taken
  everything that I've got too
She's had a million old flames so to
  her you're nothin' new
She's cold as ice but you still think
  she's hot
She's got everything it takes to take
  everything you've got
She's got everything it takes to take
  everything you've got

"Signs"

WRITTEN WITH Philip Russell
UNRELEASED

Everybody's got a theory
A reputation too
We don't want to come off crazy
With something hard to chew
But it's time to get our place in line
Before it's time to call
And there's no time better than
  now
The writing's on the wall

Chorus:
Signs
All around us are these signs
You see them every day
Signs
We don't need to joke about it
Signs
Always headin' their way
Signs

I heard it on the news today
Apocalypse comes true
I close my eyes and pray
I hope he takes me too
Don't know when it's gonna be
But it'll be worldwide
Lord I'm gonna be ready
And not get left behind

[Chorus]

I know a remedy . . .
Written for you and me . . .

[Repeat chorus]

"So Lonesome and Blue"

UNRELEASED

I'm so lonesome and blue
No one to tell my troubles to
I've got nothing left to lose
Since I lost you
That ole moon up in the sky
Don't even know the reason why
That you left me all alone and so
    blue
Them dog-gone blues I got 'em bad
Takes all the love I ever had
All the sorrow that I bear
Don't have no one to even care
That ole moon up in the sky
Don't even know the reason why
That you left me all alone and so
    blue
This ole heart of mine is cursed
It just goes from bad to worse
Lord I've cried me a river maybe
    two
Ain't worn a smile since don't know
    when
Probably never will again
Since you left me all alone and so
    blue
Them dog-gone blues I got 'em bad
Takes all the love I've ever had
All the sorrow that I bear
Don't have no one to even care
That ole moon up in the sky
Don't even know the reason why
That you left me all alone and so
    blue
That ole moon up in the sky
Don't even know the reason why
That you left me all alone and so
    blue

"Something You'll Never Own"

UNRELEASED

You gave me a mansion
But what I wanted was your love
You kept me in diamonds
But you kept me from your touch
You would run around all over town
While I stayed all alone
When I leave I'll leave with nothing
But I'm something you'll never own

When I leave I'll leave with nothing
But my pride
Happiness is something
Your money could never buy
All I ask for was your love
But you sold that long ago
When I leave I'll leave with nothing
But I'm something you'll never own

My love can't be bought
Like some women that you know
I'm not a prize
I'm your wife
Not for sell or for show
You say I'm a fool to leave you
Well darlin' that may be so
When I leave I'll leave with nothing
But I'm something you'll never own

"Spilled Milk"

UNRELEASED

She looks like an angel in her gown
    of white silk
As she goes to the kitchen for a
    glass of warm milk
She spills a little and commences
    to cry
Hoping I don't know the real reason
    why

Chorus:
I said: Honey, don't cry over spilled
    milk
Or the stain that it leaves on the
    silk
It can be cleaned and look good as
    new
And no one will know except me
    and you

This morning I served her her
    breakfast in bed
After I kissed her she just hung her
    head
While creaming her coffee she
    spilled the milk
And cried when some got on her
    favorite quilt

Chorus:
I said: Honey, don't cry over spilled
    milk
After all it is only a quilt
It can be cleaned and look good as
    new
And no one will know except me
    and you

She's paying dearly—
So my hurt mustn't show
I love her too much to let her know
    I know

"Sometimes I Wish I'd Let Him Love Me"

WRITTEN WITH Bobby Tomberlin and
Lorene Allen
UNRELEASED

You always thought this friend of
    ours was just a friend
But sometimes when you'd hurt
    me, I'd often turn to him
I can look you in the eye and say
    I've always been faithful to you
If I had to do it all over, I can't say
    I'd be true

Chorus:
Sometimes I wish I'd let him love
    me
When I know you don't care
When you act like I'm not here
What are we together for
I never hear I Love You anymore
He told me many times
What happiness we could find
But I never was the kind to be
    untrue
Sometimes I wish I'd let him love
    me away from you

Now it's too late for what might've
    been
Nothing but a memory remains of
    him
I couldn't take the chance it
    would've torn our worlds apart

Though you were taking me for granted
While he took me to heart

"Still Woman Enough"

UNRELEASED

Well I've been through some bad times
Been on the bottom
Been at the top
And I've seen life from both sides
It's what you make with what you've got
There's been times that life's got me down

Picked myself up and bounced right back around
I wasn't raised to give up
And to this day you know what
I'm still woman enough
Still got what it takes inside
I know how to love lose and survive
Ain't much I ain't seen and I ain't tried
I've been knocked down but never out of the fight
I'm strong but I'm tender
Wise but I'm tough
And let me tell you when it comes to love
I'm still woman enough
Well I was borned in old Kentucky
Hey I'm country
And proud to say

And I've seen a lot of changes
Oh but I ain't never changed
Yeah this here girl's been there
    done that
They call me hillbilly
I got the last laugh
Standing here today
Proving in every way
I'm still woman enough
Still got what it takes inside
I know how to love lose and survive
Ain't much I ain't seen and I ain't
    tried
I've been knocked down but never
    out of the fight
I'm strong but I'm tender
Wise but I'm tough
And let me tell you when it comes
    to love
I'm still woman enough
The years may come and go
But to me it's just time
'Cause without a doubt I know
It ain't your age it's a state of mind
Hahaha
I'm still woman enough
Still got what it takes inside
I know how to love lose and survive
Ain't much I ain't seen and I ain't
    tried
I've been knocked down but never
    out of the fight
I'm strong but I'm tender
Wise but I'm tough
And let me tell you when it comes
    to love
I'm still woman enough
I'm still woman enough
I'm still woman enough
I'm still woman enough
Still woman enough—I'm still
    woman enough

"Thank God for Jesus"

WRITTEN WITH Shawn Camp
UNRELEASED

Thank God for Jesus
Thank God for Jesus
Let's praise His love with all our
    hearts and
Thank God for Jesus
Get down upon your knees and
    pray and
Thank God for Jesus
Thank God for Jesus

Remember when the rain comes
    down
To thank God for Jesus
Let's raise our voices to the clouds
And thank God for Jesus

He (God) destroyed the world with
    a mighty flood
Left nonbelievers stuck in the mud
Then He gave us a rainbow to show
    His love
Oh, thank God for Jesus
Whoa, thank God for Jesus

Let's tell the world of this great
    man
And thank God for Jesus
Without Him we don't have a
    chance
So, thank God for Jesus

If you go to heaven gotta go
    through Him
That's the way that it's always been
He'll deliver you from sin
So, thank God for Jesus

OPPOSITE Loretta with
Luciano Pavarotti, 1983

193

Solo:

Thank God for Jesus
Thank God for Jesus
Let's raise our hands and praise the
    Lord and
Thank God for Jesus
Lawdy He's the one I'm shoutin' for
Thank God for Jesus

If I look happy don't you
    understand
Jesus has me by the hand
And He's leadin' me to the
    promised land
Yeah, thank God for Jesus
Thank God for Jesus

Let's praise His love with all our
    hearts and
Thank God for Jesus
Get down upon your knees and
    pray and
Thank God for Jesus
Thank God for Jesus

Amen . . .

"That Pleading Look"

WRITTEN WITH Teddy Wilburn
UNRELEASED

I've died a thousand times these
    last few months I've lived with
    you.
I know there's nothing left, yet I
    feel sorry for you, too.
My mind's been set on leavin', then
    my heart would start believin'

That pleading look, there in your
    eyes.

That pleading look had made me
    stay,
The times I'd want to run away.
Could it be that's just a front you're
    puttin' on?
The cruel weeds you are sowin'
Seem to die when I start goin'.
And there's that pleading look
    there in your eyes.

That pleading look won't work this
    time,
My heart has just made up its mind,
And your pleading eyes can walk
    me to the door.
I've watched love finish dyin',
So I'll be too busy cryin',
To see that pleading look there in
    your eyes.

"There Ain't No Woman Enough to Take Your Man"

UNRELEASED

Oh don't believe this woman that's
    tellin' you these things,
I've only seen her once or twice and
    hardly know her name,
Please darlin' listen, and try to
    understand,
That there ain't no woman enough
    to take your man.

She could never be the woman you
   are,
They don't make 'em anymore
And you must know I love you
   'cause you're all I'm livin' for
So don't worry 'bout her honey,
   trespassin' on your land
'Cause there ain't no woman
   enough to take your man.

What makes you think I'd look at
   her when there's nothin' there to
   see,
That painted face that she wears
   don't mean a thing to me,
There ain't no one that gets to me
   just the way you can,
And there ain't no woman enough
   to take your man.

She could never be the woman you
   are,
They don't make 'em anymore
And you must know I love you
   'cause you're all I'm livin' for
So don't worry 'bout her honey,
   trespassin' on your land
'Cause there ain't no woman
   enough to take your man.

"There's the Door"

WRITTEN WITH Patsy Lynn Russell
UNRELEASED

I thought our love was built on
   strong foundation
Till I found out I was knee deep in
   sand
I opened up the windows to my
   heart

But you just closed them
When you cheated and you lied
It all hit the fan

I've been walking the floor
While you've been running
But I'm not gonna do that anymore
It's easy as one two three
And see ya later
You hurt me bad I'm through with
   you
There's the door

Please don't stand there like a rock
That just stopped rollin'
'Cause leaving me is something
You know how to do
Just take a look around this room
'Cause it's the last time you'll ever
   see it painted blue

"To Save My Soul"

UNRELEASED

Well there comes a million
   memories through the door
Here I go runnin' back
To make me just one more
Lord I lost all sense of shame
I've completely lost control
And I can't save my heart to save
   my soul

Baby what do you see in her
That you can't see in me
She ain't got nothing I ain't got
I'm more of a woman than she'll
   ever be

OPPOSITE Loretta with
Ray Charles

If I lose control I'll lose my heart,
  mind and soul
But I can't save my heart to save my
  soul

Well she can't love you like I can
Don't you know that baby
Our love's worth more than gold
My man is one thing she can't hold
And I can't lose control
Oh I can't save my heart to save my
  soul

"Turn Off the Heat"

UNRELEASED

Well you want me to be a good girl
That's the way I want to be
But lately your fun's gettin' just a
  little
Too friendly with me
You know how much I love you
And I would never cheat
If you want to play it cool
Turn off the heat

You say you couldn't have a girl
That had done something bad
And doing, doing wrong
Is something this girl never had
You say these things, but you've
  tried
Everything, as soon as our lives
  meet
If you want to play it cool
Turn off the heat

'Cause if you want to play it cool
Turn off the heat
You got to know your arms
Are making this girl weak
If you're looking for a good girl
That's never been loved you see
If you want to play it cool
You better turn off the heat

"Waitin' on You to Make Up Your Heart"

WRITTEN WITH The Lynns
UNRELEASED

You say you love me then you say
  you don't
You always will, but then you won't
Your kind of lovin' is makin' me
  blue
I don't know why I jus' don't turn
  you loose
Instead of sittin' around here
  watchin' the clock
Waitin' on you to make up your
  heart

Chorus:
 Hey now baby
It's always maybe
Like a fool I'm stuck in the dark
Waitin' on you to make up your
  heart

What's all this stallin', honey make
  up your mind
What's the problem, stop wasting
  my time

My sense of humor is not amused
Can't understand why you're so
confused
I'll probably wind up in an old
graveyard
Waitin' on you to make up your
heart

[Repeat chorus]

[First verse repeats]

[Repeat chorus]

"Wanted Man"

UNRELEASED

Well girl I see what you're lookin' at
If I were you I wouldn't do that
It will get you in trouble
That you can't get out of
If you slip and fall you're gonna go
down hard
There's more to cheatin'
Than just playin' cards
He's a wanted man
He's a wanted man

With Roy Orbison

The Recording Academy
honors Loretta Lynn,
with Dawn Hull, Chairman
of the Recording Academy
George Flanigen, and
Reba McEntire, 2011

Yeah he's a wanted man
So you'd better leave him alone
He's got two little babies who call
   him Daddy at home
He's a wanted man
Yeah and it's my place to tell you
   this
Girl I'm his Mrs. not his Miss
And he's a wanted man
He's a wanted man

If I were you I'd turn around and run
Find someone else and have your
   fun
You're gonna get in trouble
That you can't get out of
You may think he'll go easy
But to get to him
You'll have to go through me
He's a wanted man
He's a wanted man

Yeah he's a wanted man
So you better leave him alone
He's got two little babies who call
   him Daddy at home
He's a wanted man
Yeah and it's my place to tell you
   this
I'm his Mrs. not his Miss
And he's a wanted man
He's a wanted man

"We Ain't Got a Prayer (If We Don't Pray)"

WRITTEN WITH Shawn Camp
UNRELEASED

I'm on my knees
With my face to the ground

And I'll stay right here
'Til I feel that I've been found
Lord don't let the devil
Keep standin' in my way
'Cause we ain't got a prayer
If we don't pray
No we ain't got a prayer if we don't
   pray
And I'll be down on my knees as
   long as I have to stay
I'm on the narrow path and I'm
   determined not to sway
'Cause we ain't got a prayer if we
   don't pray
The road's so rough
And rocky here below
And we all wanna walk
Upon those streets of gold
If we just keep on sinnin'
I'm afraid we won't be saved
'Cause we ain't got a prayer
If we don't pray
No we ain't got a prayer if we don't
   pray
And I'll be down on my knees as
   long as I have to stay
I'm on the narrow path and I'm
   determined not to sway
'Cause we ain't got a prayer if we
   don't pray
So put your hands together
And thank Him for the price He paid
'Cause we ain't got a prayer if we
   don't pray
No, we ain't got a prayer if we don't
   pray

Loretta Lynn's
Greatest Hits

.MCA RECORDS

MCA-935

SUCCESS

DEAR UNCLE SAM

BLUE KENTUCKY GIRL

THE HOME YOU'RE TEARIN DOWN

BEFORE I'M OVER YOU

HAPPY BIRTHDAY

YOU AIN'T WOMAN ENOUGH

WINE WOMEN AND SONG

DON'T COME HOME A 'DRINKIN'

THE OTHER WOMAN

IF YOU'RE NOT GONE TOO LONG

She's a master class in song-writing, and I've always been in love with the teacher.

DEL BRYANT

"What's It Gonna Take"

WRITTEN WITH The Lynns
UNRELEASED

What's it gonna take to stop lovin'
    you
I've asked myself a million times
What more can you put me through
You've been nothing but a
    heartache
Right from the very start
So I can't understand why leavin' is
    so hard
What's it gonna take to stop lovin'
    you

Oh what's it gonna take to finally
    realize
Your love ain't worth the pain you
    put me through
If I could just convince my heart
To break these chains that bind
And somehow find the strength to
    turn you loose
What's it gonna take to stop lovin'
    you

How far do you have to go
For me to face the truth 'cause all
    the love I've given
Baby you've just abused
How much more is my heart
Willing to endure
Is it gonna take a miracle
Only God knows for sure
What's it gonna take to stop lovin'
    you

Oh what's it gonna take to finally
    realize

Your love ain't worth the pain you
    put me through
If I could just convince my heart
To break these chains that bind
And somehow find the strength to
    turn you loose
What's it gonna take to stop lovin'
    you

"What Kind of Fool"

WRITTEN WITH The Lynns
UNRELEASED

I vowed to love you for the rest of
    my life
But when I gave my heart to you I
    never closed my eyes
So what makes you think that I've
    grown blind that I don't see
The only one that kept that promise
    in this love's been me

What kind of a fool have you taken
    me for
If you're lookin' to be free, that's
    what you got in store
What kind of a man slips a promise
    off his left hand
Pretends it's not there no more
What kind of a fool have you taken
    me for

I've been faithful to you baby can
    you say the same
'Cause these tears that's rollin'
    down my face bear your name
And I will step aside before I let you
    step on me

So I'm not quite the fool you're
 makin' me out to be

[Chorus]

Don't try and tell me that I'm crazy
Don't try and tell me that I'm
 wrong
Baby you're the one that betrayed
 me
So don't you pretend I don't know
 what's goin' on

"Who's Gonna Miss Me When I'm Gone"

UNRELEASED

Is there one troubled soul
These hands of mine could hold
Who's gonna miss me when I'm
 gone
Who's gonna wanna follow
In my footsteps maybe
Who's gonna miss me when I'm
 gone
Who's gonna miss me tell me
Who's gonna miss me Lordy
Who's gonna miss me when I'm
 gone
If I could do one good thing
Then it won't be all in vain
Who's gonna miss me when I'm
 gone

Don't wanna move an ocean
Just tryin' to do my portion
Who's gonna miss me when I'm
 gone
Who's gonna miss me tell me
Who's gonna miss me Lordy
Who's gonna miss me when I'm
 gone
If I've made someone smile
Or just one life worthwhile
Who's gonna miss me when I'm
 gone
If there's one thing I've done
I'd like to know I've left someone
Who's gonna miss me when I'm
 gone
Who's gonna miss me tell me
Who's gonna miss me Lordy
Who's gonna miss me when I'm
 gone
Who's gonna miss me tell me
Who's gonna miss me Lordy
Who's gonna miss me when I'm
 gone
Who's gonna miss me tell me
Who's gonna miss me Lordy
Who's gonna miss me when I'm
 gone
Who's gonna miss me tell me
Who's gonna miss me Lordy
Who's gonna miss me when I'm
 gone

"Your Chief Is on the Warpath"

WRITTEN WITH Jimmy Helms
UNRELEASED

Well, in this teepee there's just one
chief,
In case you've forgotten, Squaw,
it's me.
I'll stay out huntin' if I want to, till
daylight.
Well I left you at home to keep the
teepee clean
It's the dirtiest teepee I've ever
seen.
So your chief is on the warpath
tonight.

Well I found out that you believe,
The game I'm huntin' for ain't beef
Just goes to show that Squaw you
ain't too bright.
It ain't so easy spendin' every night
out
A moonlightin' just to feed your
mouth!
Your chief is on the warpath
tonight.

Well this firewater that I've been
drinkin'
Keeps me going, but I've been
thinkin'
Just like in the movie, I'm losin' the
fight
I'm tired of bringin' out that ole
peace pipe.
I guess I'd rather split the blanket
than fight
Now, your chief is on the warpath
tonight.

"Wounded Hearts"

WRITTEN WITH The Lynns
UNRELEASED

He's a lover that I used to know
I knew you saw that in my eyes
But that old flame that once burned
so strong
Has now turned as cold as ice
I never meant to put this on you
God knows I've got no right
Baby believe me it's you
I turn to when I turn out the lights

Don't you know time heals and
wounded hearts grow strong
Time heals and wounded hearts go
on
And they get stronger by the
heartache
Stronger by the heartbreak and the
love goes on

I know you're feeling a little turned
away
We've all made our mistakes
Mine just showed up and I had a
little hurt now but time is gonna
heal
And this blanket of heartaches are
gonna lift and love again

"You Show Me Yours"

WRITTEN WITH Philip Russell
UNRELEASED

Won't you come and ride along
  with me little darlin'
Full moon's rising and the crickets
  are callin'
The starlit night will promise a
  good time
You show me yours and I'll show
  you mine

Well I don't know about that hun I
  like neon lights
Jukebox country and dance hall
  nights
But you and I could sing a song and
  we'd have us a time
You show me yours and I'll show
  you mine

Chorus:
You show me yours
And I'll show you mine
Get your head out of the gutter
  man
And straighten up this time
Better be on your toes when the
  spotlight shine
You show me yours and I'll show
  you mine

There ain't no sense in sittin' home
  alone sweet thing
We can go honky tonk like no one's
  ever dreamed
We might just get the nerve and
  twirl around the floor one time
You show me yours and I'll show
  you mine

[Chorus]

Well it's been a while and I like your
  style but I always did you know
I'm glad we called and got involved
  in this little episode
It's sure been great but it's gettin'
  late let's leave this joint behind
You show me yours and I'll show
  you mine

[Chorus]

"You've Made Me What I Am"

WRITTEN WITH Oliver Doolittle Lynn
UNRELEASED

You say that I'm no angel oh I know
it much too well
How can you look into my eyes and
ask me why I fell.
You know that I still love you and I
let you drag me down
How can you talk about me when
you've made me what I am

You've made me what I am but look
who everybody blames
When you know you're the reason I
hang my head in shame
Oh you tell me to forget you and to
stop my hangin' round
I'd be ashamed if I were you you've
made me what I am

You never really loved me but I
found that out too late
I've tried to find the way to change
my love for you to hate
You act like you don't know me
when there's someone else
around
How can you hold your head up
when you've made me what I am

You've made me what I am . . .

"Ships Still Come In"

WRITTEN WITH Lorene Allen
RELEASE DATE 1994
ALBUM Independent

Chorus:
Ships still come in don't they baby
I've not lost the faith understand
I believe everything that you've
told me
I just need to hear it once again

Tell me again our ship will come in
Sing red sails in the sunset for me
You've always told me our dreams
will come true
Oh, but darling, do you know when
that will be

Chorus:
Ships still come in don't they baby
I've not lost the faith understand
I believe everything that you've
told me
I just need to hear it once again

Bridge:
I know it's so
And I'll go where you go
Hold me close and tell me one more
time

[Chorus]

OPPOSITE Loretta and
Mooney, 1982

"Sweet Daddy Come On Home"

WRITTEN WITH Charles W. Aldridge
UNRELEASED
ALBUM *Loretta Lynn's Greatest Hits*

Well, I'm not the kind of woman to
   let her man go roamin',
Still I let you sometimes all alone,
But remember you're mine when
   you see them dangerous signs,
It's time, yeah, it's time to come on
   home.

Come on home, come on home,
Sweet daddy, it's time to come on
   home.

When you're settin' in a tavern and
   a beer you're a havin',
And you're not too sure of all that's
   goin' on,

When your head's feelin' funny and
   you're runnin' out of money,
It's time yeah, it's time to come on
   home.

Come on home, come on home,
Sweet daddy, it's time to come on
   home.

When the bar starts a tiltin' and
   your tonsils start a liltin'
When some gal's givin' you the old
   come-on
When you're admiring the beauty
   of some mini-skirted cutie
It's time yeah, it's time to come on
   home.

Come on home, come on home,
Sweet daddy, it's time to come on
   home.

I've got the kind of lovin' that will
   keep us turtle-dovin'
My love is yours and yours all alone
When you're hungry for some
   kissin', come on home for what
   you're missin'
It's time yeah it's time to come on
   home.

Come on home, come on home,
Sweet daddy, it's time to come on
   home.

"Your Cow's Gonna Get Out"

WRITTEN WITH Jay Lee Webb
UNRELEASED

Well, I've got news for you, mister,
   when you speak to me don't
   shout
You let your pond go dry and your
   fence fall down
And you're the dog that drove her
   out.

She came grazin' in my pasture, she
   was starved for love no doubt
If you leave your gate wide open
   your cows are gonna get out.

If you leave your gate wide open
   your cows are gonna get out
I heard her bawlin' too many
   nights, now I know what she's
   bawlin' about.
You were putting your brand on a
   little young heifer,
Whose horns have just begun to
   sprout.
If you leave your gate wide open,
   your cows are gonna get out.

You say you stay on a cattle drive,
   you go from herd to herd
She's got sense enough to know
   that you're no cowboy
And you go from her to a her
If you leave your water on, it will
   run all night
If you don't close the spout
If you leave your gate wide open
   your cows are gonna get out.

Songwriting

I guess my life is my songbook, 'cause I only write about what I've lived. I was never one of those songwriters who could make up some story or write about something that they have not been through. If I had a bad day I would write about it. If I had a good day I would write about that. If my husband was misbehavin', we all know I would write about that! But that's just how I am. Even now I am still writing about my life, and as long as I am on this earth, I'll be filling up my songbook.

Illustration Credits

All photographs not listed are courtesy of the Loretta Lynn Foundation

page ii Photograph by Russ Harrington, courtesy of the Loretta Lynn Foundation

page vi Photograph by Erik Atkins, courtesy of the Loretta Lynn Foundation

page 33 Courtesy of MCA Records/Universal Music Group

page 60 Courtesy of MCA Records/Universal Music Group

page 66 Courtesy of MCA Records/Universal Music Group

page 69 Courtesy of MCA Records/Universal Music Group

page 80 Courtesy of MCA Records/Universal Music Group

page 86 Courtesy of MCA Records/Universal Music Group

page 100 Photograph by Erik Atkins, courtesy of the Loretta Lynn Foundation

page 108 Photograph by William Smithson, courtesy of the Loretta Lynn Foundation

page 123 Photograph by William Smithson, courtesy of the Loretta Lynn Foundation

page 141 Courtesy of MCA Records/Universal Music Group

page 145 Courtesy of The Recording Academy

page 146 Photograph by Erik Atkins, courtesy of the Loretta Lynn Foundation

page 149 Photograph by Erik Atkins, courtesy of the Loretta Lynn Foundation

page 150 Photograph by Russ Harrington, courtesy of the Loretta Lynn Foundation

page 155 Photograph by Erik Atkins, courtesy of the Loretta Lynn Foundation

page 170 Photograph by Richard Bird, courtesy of the Loretta Lynn Foundation

page 191 Photograph by Erik Atkins, courtesy of the Loretta Lynn Foundation

page 200 Photograph by Rick Diamond, courtesy of the Loretta Lynn Foundation

page 202 Courtesy of MCA Records/Universal Music Group

page 203 Courtesy of MCA Records/Universal Music Group

page 207 Photograph by Erik Atkins, courtesy of the Loretta Lynn Foundation

page 212 Photograph by Russ Harrington, courtesy of the Loretta Lynn Foundation

Index

Acknowledgments

Thank you to all the musicians, songwriters, fans, and friends. To Surefire Music, Jason and Arvemia Wilburn, Nancy Russell, Jess Rosen, Tim Cobb, Mark Marchetti, Philip Russell, Coalminer's Music, Dawn Hull, Chelsea Kempchinsky, Megan Brutto, Eric Adkins, Russ Harrington—without each and every person above, this book would never have come to be.

A NOTE ON THE TYPE

This book was set in Thesis, a typeface created by the Dutch designer Lucas de Groot (born 1963) and released in 1994 by the FontFabrik foundry in Berlin. Originally known as Parenthesis, the Thesis family of fonts is unusual in including a serif font, a sans serif font, and a "mixed" font, which all strive to harmonize the traditionally disparate styles. In spite of its idiosyncratic character mapping, Thesis attempts to provide a complete solution to text and display type design.

Composed by North Market Street Graphics, Lancaster, Pennsylvania

Printed and bound by Berryville Graphics, Berryville, Virginia

Designed by Maggie Hinders

When you hear her voice, there's just something about it that sounds real. And when you see her live, she's just so honest and so likeable. She's not putting on any front or anything. And in person, she's exactly the same way—she'll say exactly what she thinks and means, and there's always been something fresh about that. She's what country music is all about—her whole life is just an American dream-come-true. She wrote her stuff and lived it. And the adoration she gets worldwide . . . it's amazing. The same way it was with Johnny Cash. She and her music have helped give country music a real foundation.

Alan Jackson

I have been a huge fan of Loretta Lynn's as long as I can remember. One of the best days of my life was when we became friends. I have watched her perform, visit with fans, visit with her peers of country music, and in all of these places, she's always the same. *That's what I love about Loretta.* Our fans know a fake—she's not one. Our peers check you out to see that you're honest—she is. To get to spend a day with Loretta would be a dream-come-true. Like I said, I've been a fan for as long as I can remember, just like millions of others.

Reba McEntire